STONE DEAD

STONE DEAD

MARION CROOK

OVERLEA
HOUSE

Copyright © 1987 by Grolier Limited. All rights reserved. No part of this book may be reproduced or transmitted in any form or by any means, electronic or mechanical, including photography, recording, or any information storage or retrieval system, without permission in writing from the publisher.

Published by: Overlea House
Toronto, Ontario
Canada

Cover art: Alan Daniel

R.L.: Y.A.

Canadian Cataloguing in Publication Data

Crook, Marion, 1941–
 Stone dead

ISBN 0-7172-1615-2

I. Title.

PS8555.R663S76 1987   jC813'.54   C87-094460-6
PZ7.C766St 1987

1234567890   GP   6543210987

Printed and Bound in Canada

To my son Glen
to remind him of his life
as a ranch hand

CHAPTER ONE

I hadn't counted on bears. Hard work, yes. Trouble with Andrew, yes. Blisters, sore feet, fatigue and too little sleep—all these I'd thought about before I moved up to the Cariboo for the summer. But no one had warned me about the bears.

"A brown bear's been seen twice this week," Evelyn, my landlady, told me as I picked up my helmet and bike keys. "It might show up at the Ross ranch. You watch for it, Susan."

"Watch for it? Watch for it! Bears don't come near people, do they?"

"Not usually, but you can't predict what wild animals will do. This bear climbed up onto Joe Stone's porch. It has nerve." She dropped a bread roll onto the pan. "Fred said it came in from the east looking for an easy meal, and now it's waltzing all over our meadows as if it had paid the registration fee on every calf on the place. Martin saw it yesterday." She flipped a floured hand through the rest of the bread dough. "You look out this morning. That bear's a nuisance!"

"I'll do that." Bears! My stomach flipped. The only bears I'd ever seen were on TV or in a cage at the zoo—and even there, I stood far back. "What am I supposed to do if I see it?"

"You couldn't shoot it, could you?" She eyed me as if I was six instead of sixteen, and not smart.

"I've never shot anything." I don't even approve of shooting animals. What about conservation and respect for the bear's rights? For Evelyn, it was simple. If a bear bothered the cows, then someone should shoot the bear. But I wasn't sure that it was right. So why did I feel useless because I couldn't shoot one?

"Never mind, you can't know how to do everything at once. Call here and I'll send Fred or Martin over to deal with it. Try Joe Stone if he's handy."

"Joe wouldn't lift a finger to help me if the bear was ripping me to pieces."

Evelyn snorted. "I don't know if he's that lazy, but he sure doesn't do any more than he can help. That ranch of his needs nails on the barn shakes and drainage ditches in the yard. Fred would lick it into shape in two months."

"Hey, listen, Evelyn. What about the

bear? I can't handle a bear!" I was getting nervous just thinking about it. Maybe she was exaggerating.

"Oh, don't fuss. It probably won't come near you. If you see it, call here. I'll send someone to help you." She wiped the counter with one big sweep of her cloth as if she could manage the counter, the house, her family, me, the bear and God Almighty, given enough time.

My Honda 110 started on the first try and I eased it out onto the gravel road. The clatter of the engine flushed up a grouse at the side of the road. Any bear would run from the noise. The dirt bike tires took the loose gravel pretty well but slipped a little on the corners. The bike was a graduation present from my brothers. They had paid a third apiece and told me to take care but have fun. I like the power under my hands and the feel of the wind on my face. Nice guys, my brothers, even Luke, who is fifteen and sometimes silly.

It takes a few minutes to ride from Evelyn's house where I board to Andrew Ross's place where I work. I usually listen to a tape on the way, but that morning my mind was on bears and I didn't plug into my headset.

I saw a puff of dust at the top of the hill and waited as another motorbike came closer. It was Martin. I waved, and he stopped.

"How's it going?" I yelled. Neither of us got off our machines.

"Okay. Dad needs some more tools." He didn't smile. I'd never seen him smile. He had been sweating, and the dust had caked on his face and made his dark hair gray. There wasn't any place in a hay field that wasn't dusty. His jeans had a layer of road dust on them, and everything about him was a faded gray color except his bright green eyes.

"Your mom's making buns."

He nodded and kicked his machine into gear. I felt sorry for Martin. His dad never said one good thing about him or to him. I didn't have a dad anymore, but I couldn't understand constantly picking on one of your kids until he stopped talking to you, sagged at the shoulders and looked at the ground most of the time. I'd seen pictures of the two of them at a ball game, at Boy Scouts and at a 4-H rally, but Martin was much younger then. I wondered when they had stopped being friends.

I kicked my bike into first and started down the road to Andrew Ross's place.

The ranch sprawled out over the rolling hillside, the house at the top and the farm buildings toward the creek at the bottom. This was where Andrew had lived for thirty years and where my boyfriend, his son, had grown up. Allan wants to come back here some day, but he has another four years in the Royal Canadian Mounted Police before he can make any move.

Working at the ranch for the summer was a great way to get away from my mother and brothers and live on my own for a couple of months. I love my family, but when I'm home with them, I'm never sure if I make up my own mind about anything. They're always there to look after me and help me and encourage me. I wanted to get away to some place where I had to make all my decisions by myself. When Allan mentioned that his dad needed extra help on the ranch for the summer, I thought it would be just the place for me—no brothers, no mother, no boyfriend, no problems.

Allan didn't want me to go. We were drinking Coke at my house when I suggested it. He was impressive in his police uniform: hat, badges, gold trim, shiny gun and holster—the symbols of Authority and Control.

"You'd be gone all summer. Stuck up there in the boondocks, slaving away on the ranch. Everyone will be haying. Dad's a bear when he's working and Judith won't be around."

"Judith?"

"Dad's girlfriend. They're getting married in the fall sometime."

"What's she like?"

"Okay. She's a community health nurse, a couple of years younger than Dad. She's okay. Sharp."

"Where's she going?" I hadn't heard

about Judith before and I was curious.

"She has to work in the south Cariboo. Taking a supervisor's place or something. So there won't be anyone there for you to talk to. There won't be any fun for you at all and I'll be down here. And you'll have to work too hard. Dad's into sheep this year. He hates sheep, so he'll have you looking after them."

"Why? I mean why does he hate sheep?"

Allan shrugged. "Who knows?"

"Okay, if he hates sheep, why does he have them?"

"The price of hay went down; the price of lamb went up. Dad's a farmer, but he's a businessman too. If sheep make money, he'll get into sheep. Hey, think again, Susan. Be reasonable."

By "reasonable," he meant, "Look at it my way." He didn't want me on that ranch this summer; he wanted me in Chilliwack helping my mother in the grocery store—agreeable and handy. I had other ideas.

At first Andrew Ross didn't want to hire me. But I told him about the government incentive plan that would pay most of my wages. Andrew likes to save a dollar. I also said I'd make his supper every night and leave it hot for him.

That did it. I got the job. I would be mending fences, feeding animals and generally doing all the chores he didn't have time for in haying season.

My mom approved of my summer job.

"Great idea! You'll know whether you can take all that isolation, all that great outdoors, all that work! And really, Susan, you are a lot more independent than you'll admit. Maybe you'll find that out for yourself this summer."

I'm making enough money to cover my board at Evelyn's and save for pilot training at flight school. So this is a practical plan, not just a need to prove myself. I have ambitions—I want to be an airline pilot. At least I think I do. Even if I end up getting married or something, I want to try flying.

Of course, I might not like it. I might decide to do something entirely different. Even farm in the Cariboo. That's what Allan wants me to do eventually. He's a few years older than me and he has his life all planned: stay with the RCMP until his dad retires then take over the ranch. Me, I guess I don't know what I really want. Maybe away from Allan and my family, I'll have a chance to find out.

CHAPTER TWO

So far, I didn't mind the work—I'd worked just as hard at basketball and field hockey—but in spite of Allan's warning, I hadn't really expected to be alone so much. By now I knew what to do, so unless there was an extra job Andrew had to tell me about, I worked alone until suppertime.

Andrew's truck was gone when I pulled into his yard. He was probably out in the hay field.

I leaned my Honda against the house and pocketed the key—a city habit. No one here bothered to take the keys out.

While everyone else got the hay in, I looked after all the animals on the ranch. I had looked forward to feeding the animals, but doing it was something else. I'd imagined myself gracefully throwing grain to a circle of barnyard hens. I'd never imagined the rooster.

I picked up a stick and a bucket full of chicken pellets, took a deep breath and pushed open the hen house door.

He was waiting for me. The minute I got inside, that big white rooster flew at me screaming, spurs forward, wings flapping. I cracked him with the stick and he dropped to the ground. I dumped the grain and felt in the nests for eggs. All the time I watched the rooster. He was an ugly dirty-white color with muddy brown speckles, and when he spread his wings in attack, he looked huge. He shook himself, then flew up to the first roost and adjusted his feet on the rungs. I put the last egg in the bucket and faced him. He came at me again. I missed him with the stick this time and dodged away. He landed at my feet, so I kicked him and darted out the door. Honestly! He didn't attack anyone but me. Andrew went in there, Martin went in there, even Evelyn went in there, and the stupid rooster just looked at them. How could a rooster hate one particular person?

The pigs were another problem. When I first came to the farm I thought that pigs were small, white, gentle animals. I wasn't prepared for Sharon—half a ton of greed that shifted and rooted around the pen. If she ever got out she would root up the ground like a rototiller and eat everything she could find, including the chickens. The first day I was here a hen flew into the pigpen. In two seconds that hen disappeared down Sharon's throat—bones, feathers and meat all crunched in a couple of grinding twitches of Sharon's jaw. All that was left was a pair of yellow feet. Andrew wasn't impressed. He said that she wouldn't hurt people, but I didn't trust her. For such a big animal she was fast on her feet. I stood *outside* her pen, dumped her feed over the fence, then returned to the house.

I put the eggs in the back porch and picked up the slop bucket half full of potato peelings, old apples, stale bread and uneaten porridge. I'd saved these treats for the little pigs, Bernie, Ruth and Sampson, who lived in a small pen next to the barn under the hayloft door. These pigs I liked. They were the size of cocker spaniels and friendly. I'd just closed the door when Andrew's truck crunched into the driveway.

"What broke down this time?"

He climbed out of the cab—dusty jeans, dusty shirt, dusty dark gray beard. "A couple of teeth on the mower. I have spares with me, but I left the wrench in the porch." He pushed open the door and reached in for the wrench. No "Good morning." No "How are you?" Nice guy.

"Evelyn said to watch out for a bear."

Andrew stopped and looked at me. "You'd better have the rifle handy."

"Hey. This is me. What do I know about a rifle?" But he ignored that and brushed past me into the house, returning in a moment with a long, brown rifle. He leaned it against the wall inside the porch.

"What am I supposed to do with that?"

"Are you daft? Use it. The bullets are on the windowsill."

I stared at him.

"Ach! Useless, are you? Call the Lees' place if you can't do it. Someone will come. If you can't get your wits together, just point the rifle up in the air and shoot. That ought to scare anything off."

"All right. I might be able to do that."

"Now out of my way, girl, and don't waste any more of my time. I've got four men I'm paying by the hour waiting for me in the field."

"I wouldn't dream of wasting your time. Go."

None of my brothers ever acted like that. Andrew gave orders all the time. He was always telling me what to do. He seemed to think that I couldn't get anything right.

Andrew dropped the wrench into the back of the truck where it bounced once against the metal side.

"Mind the pigs," he said. He had to have the last word.

I wished I'd contracted to work for someone who was more understanding, someone who had a sense of humor and who liked me or at least talked to me. I ground my teeth together in the back. My dentist tells me I'll wear them out if I don't stop that. I forced my jaw muscles to relax and concentrated on letting the tension go from my facial muscles.

I picked up the slop bucket and started toward the barn. The green meadows stretched to the fir forest beyond the last fence where tall trees spiked the blue sky. The morning heat would bring a haze later, but right now the air was clear and the sky that brilliant cobalt blue of postcards. I was going to get up into that sky. I was going to fly. I was going to open my life to a new dimension of power and freedom. I was going to move into another world. If Andrew continued to treat me like some sort of feudal slave, I might even do it soon.

I was thinking so hard about swooping through the air in a fast plane that I was up the ladder to the hayloft before I realized that I still had the slop bucket in my hand. I put it down by the ladder so I wouldn't forget to take it around later and searched the hayloft for eggs. The barn hens sometimes hide eggs in the hay bales, and if no one finds them, they rot there.

The loft was quiet, warm and sleepy, full of hay bales and dust. I sneezed, then listened for the little pigs. I heard a couple of snuffles and grunts, then suddenly high-pitched squeals and a scream. I ran to the hayloft door, gripped the wall and looked down.

The bear was inside the pigpen right below me. Two pigs were dead. Ripped apart. The third had scrambled to the far corner and was trying to hide under the fence. The bear ignored it. The top of his head was right below me—not an arm's reach away. He reared up on his back legs, lifted his head and stared straight at me. I stared back and froze.

The bear moved his head in a slow arc, swayed and then dropped to all fours. He hooked one of the pigs with his claws, rolled over the fence and loped off dragging it with him. The surviving pig went crazy. It squealed in terror and tore around the pen. I stood very still. If I had walked around the barn to feed the pigs before searching for eggs, I'd have walked right into that bear. Prickles shivered down my arms. I swallowed. My knees shook and I sat down on a bale.

The bear was gone, halfway to the forest and making good time over the pasture grass.

Ruth, the last pig, continued to squeal. She was doing what I wanted to do, running wildly and screaming. Both of us were waiting for the bear to come back. Would he come into the barn and get me? Could he get up into the hayloft? Could he climb the ladder? He knew I was here. I took a deep breath.

I wasn't going to wait for trouble. I jumped to my feet and checked at the hayloft door. No sign of the bear. I slid down the ladder and ran to the house. If there was a bear in the yard, I'd never have seen it; I ran as if I was wired with rockets.

The rifle was still leaning against the porch wall, the bullets on the windowsill. How did you load this thing? I stood by the back door of the house and studied the mechanism. Slowly I pushed three bullets into the empty space. I pulled the bolt back and watched the first bullet slide into place. Good. Now I had to hide, but not far from the house. There was no place in the yard—no tree, no wagon, no car. Finally I slid behind a big water barrel at the far side of the house. From there I had a good view of the meadow and the pigpen. That bear would be back. I knew he would be back. He was not going to get Ruth. I waited.

CHAPTER THREE

The only shooting I'd ever done was some target shooting with my brothers, and we'd used .22 rifles. You aimed and pulled the trigger. Simple.

I waited an hour and got a cramp in my leg. I pushed my toes hard on the ground, trying to work the pain out of the muscle. If the bear didn't come back, I was wasting the whole morning. Andrew would be mad if I didn't get that broken fence fixed today.

Dust puffed behind the chickens as they pecked and scratched in the dirt, searching compulsively for bits of food. The sun reflected off the house wall behind me and radiated heat. It was hard to stay alert in the warmth and the quiet. Two chickens rose into the air feathers flapping, shrieking and complaining to each other, then settled back to their constant hunt for food. Sheep bells tinkled from the east pasture. A Gray Jay swooped over the yard and hopped up onto the back porch, looking for scraps from the pig slop.

Everything seemed normal, peaceful. Then just when I'd decided I wasn't going to stay another minute, I saw something move in the lower meadow. At first it was a flicker at the edge of my sight, then a shadow, then a definite shape moving fast up the hill to the barn. I swallowed, concentrated on my hands and slowly moved the gun into position to cover the pigpen. The bear moved up to the fence, stood on his hind legs and sniffed the air.

Ruth was screaming again, high-pitched hysterical screams. I brought the gun to my shoulder and sighted along the barrel. The bear wasn't far away—I could see him clearly through the sights—but I didn't know where to aim. His head would be best, but it was small and I might miss. His heart must be in the middle somewhere.

"Squeeze the trigger slowly," my brothers had told me. Slowly I squeezed. The noise was louder than I'd expected, shattering; it filled my head. The gun kicked into my shoulder, jerked out of my hands and spun onto the ground. The bear roared a loud, huffing bellow, tumbled onto the grass and rushed across the meadow. His back legs chased his front ones as he almost flew into the trees at the bottom of the hill.

I stood beside the water barrel and stared

at the empty meadow. Such a hunter! Such a great hunter! I put the gun back against the wall inside the porch and phoned Evelyn.

"All right, Susan. No one really expected you to hit it."

"Oh, well . . . maybe not. But I don't want it to come back here."

"It won't. You've probably scared it into the next district."

"Are you sure?"

"Naturally."

"It was huge."

"They are."

"It killed two of the pigs."

"Bears do that."

"Hey, Evelyn! It was scary."

"Yes, I suppose it was. You'd better get on with your work. Andrew won't thank you for standing around."

"Okay, okay."

Standing around! I'd saved Ruth from the bear. That took *some* time.

I hung up the phone carefully, making sure I didn't slam it and walked out Andrew's back door toward the barn. Ruth cowered in the corner of the pigpen, but otherwise she was all right.

I leaned over the fence for a moment. "You owe me one, Ruth." No one else was going to think I was a hero.

The fencing pliers and the staples—horseshoe-shaped nails—were on the bench. Andrew had shown me how to fix the fence and insisted that I do it precisely as he had instructed. Fussy.

In the near meadow, two strands of barbed wire dipped over the gaping smooth wire squares of the sheep fence. I hooked the fencing pliers on the lower strand of smooth wire and pulled. When the wire was taut, I took the staple from my teeth, pressed it into the wooden pole, prayed it would stay there, grabbed the hammer and hit it. Often the staple fell before I could hit it and I'd have to do it again. Sometimes again and again. This would have been easier with two people—or one person with three hands—but I stuck with it and managed to get the sheep wire on so that it looked good, even if it wasn't as tight as Andrew wanted.

My Walkman was in my packsack but today I hadn't brought it to the meadow with me. If I were listening to music out here, I wouldn't hear a bear creeping up on me. The meadow had its own everyday sounds that kept me anxious: twigs snapping, trees brushing against each other. I turned my head every five minutes to find out what was causing the noises. Nothing. Just the fence, the meadow and me.

I ran out of staples. I suppose Andrew had left enough staples to do the fence if he had been doing it, but dozens of them had disappeared into the long grass when I missed with the hammer. It wasn't easy. I trudged back to the barn, watching the edge of the woods, turning suddenly once when a woodpecker banged its beak against a dead tree.

Ruth still huddled in the far corner of the pigpen, but she was quiet.

I searched the barn. No more staples. None on the bench, none on the shelves. I checked the back porch of the house. Lambing supplies, veterinary medicine. No staples.

Two strands of barbed wire still dipped over my tight sheep fence. Andrew wouldn't like it.

Joe Stone's place was closer than Evelyn's. He might have staples. I kicked my Honda alive and headed for the main road.

Noise, wonderful noise! No bear would come anywhere near a noisy engine like this one. The vibrations rattled the bones in my hands, traveled up my arms and shook my body. It felt great. Comforting. Normal. The sun warmed my shoulders and I felt myself relax. The bear would stay away. Evelyn knew this country. She was probably right.

The gray car came at me so fast I only had time to stare at it and then react with a quick sideways twist that sent me teetering on the edge of the ditch. I felt the rush of wind on my side. "The wind from a passing car will draw you to it," I could hear my brother Joe saying in my mind. "Head away from the car to compensate." I concentrated on steering toward the ditch so that I could keep a straight line at the edge. Then as soon as the rush of air had passed me, I turned the handlebars back toward the road. Safe. Man. Crazy driver. I slowed to a stop and looked back down the road, but the car was gone.

In that second before I reacted I had seen the license plate. SEG, my initials, Susan Elizabeth George. I didn't remember the numbers, but I remembered the letters as clearly as if they were hanging in the air in front of me.

I took a couple of deep breaths. Close. The ditch beside me was deep, with two big, gray rocks at the bottom. Really close. I rolled some gas into the motor and took the last section of the road to Joe's place at a slow and careful pace.

He wasn't home. I knocked three times, then pushed his kitchen door open and stuck my head in.

"Joe! Are you here?"

No answer. What a messy house! Dishes everywhere. Pots on the stove. Papers on the floor. Yuck! I bet he kept garbage in here for weeks. I sniffed the air. Flowers? The place was dirty, but it smelled of flowers. I didn't see any, but he might have some in another room. Joe? Putting flowers in his house? I don't think so. I shrugged and hurried out the door. That fence wasn't going to repair itself.

"Joe!" I yelled at the empty yard. He was probably haying or in town getting parts for the haying equipment. I'd help myself to staples; Andrew could pay for them or square it somehow later. People in this district always borrowed one another's farming supplies. Andrew kept his staples in the barn. Maybe that's where Joe kept his. It was worth a try.

I had to shove Joe's barn door to get in. The bottom of the door dragged on the floor. You could see that it had dragged for years because there was a groove in the floor. Why hadn't he fixed it? I suppose he never fixed a thing until he absolutely had to. At first I couldn't see anything because my eyes were used to bright sunlight. I blinked and waited a moment. The light switch by the door didn't work. I wasn't surprised. I hesitated, trying to make out shapes. Under the high window, I could see a long bench crowded with cans and heaps of nails. Would the staples be in the cans? There were piles of old bolts and pieces of machinery, some square shiny boxes that looked like radios and there, at the end of the bench, an odd shape that looked like a hand.

"Joe?" Maybe it was a glove. I moved toward it and brushed against a cobweb hanging in the air. I swatted at it. String. I pulled and light filled the barn.

It was a hand all right. It was Joe Stone's hand. He had fallen back against the bench, his hand outflung, a huge hole in his chest.

I screamed—a wild, barn-raising scream.

CHAPTER FOUR

I was out in the sunlight before I did any thinking at all. My bike! There it was. I grabbed the handlebars and pushed it onto the driveway. Now the key. It was in my pocket. Somewhere. I searched through every pocket twice before I finally found it. I would not think about what was in the barn. I would not think about it. I had to get back to Andrew's place.

And then the motor wouldn't start. Once. Twice. Three times. Finally!

Sharp stones hit my knees as my wheels spun in the gravel on the corner. Slow down, Susan. Don't kill yourself. Death. That's what I'd seen. Death. Don't think about it now. Just drive.

No one was at Andrew's house when I arrived. I don't know why I expected someone to be there. Someone to take care of me, to tell me everything was going to be all right.

It was only when I realized that I was alone, that there was no one to tell me what to do—no mother, no brothers, no Allan—that I let myself think about what had happened. The edge of my vision started to blur and everything seemed to travel away from me. I sat down suddenly with my head between my knees. I would not faint. I would *not* faint. There were bears around here, and murderers. I couldn't afford to be unconscious.

The world tipped, balanced, settled back into the familiar landscape. A sheep bleated from the near meadow. Then all was quiet.

I took two deep breaths, got slowly to my feet and went into Andrew's house to phone.

The woman who answered at the police station was particularly slow. I wanted to scream at her, "Think faster, talk faster, do something." But Joe was dead and the bear was gone and a few minutes delay wouldn't make any difference.

"And your name, please?"

I gave it.

"How do you spell that?"

I spelled it out for her.

"Telephone number?"

I gave it.

"Address?"

"McLeese Lake Road."

"And your complaint?"

I had to think for a moment. I wasn't really complaining about anything. "I want to report a murder."

"A murder."

"Yes."

"I see. And the name of the person murdered?"

"Joe Stone."

"Joe?" Her voice sharpened. "What happened to him?"

"Someone shot him."

"My heavens! Whereabouts?"

What did she mean?

"In the chest."

"No, I mean where is Joe's . . . uh . . . his body?"

"In his barn."

"And where are you?"

"At Andrew Ross's place."

Suddenly she was warm and real.

"Now you wait right there, honey, and I'll send an officer over to Joe's place and another one to Andrew's. They're both going to want to talk to you. Is Evelyn there?"

"No one's here but me."

"I'll send Evelyn to you. You've had quite a shock."

"No, don't send Evelyn. She's baking."

"Well . . . are you going to be all right?"

"Yes. And thanks."

I hung up the phone quickly. It had been easier for me when she was a robot. When she was kind, I started disintegrating inside to mush and shakes.

Outside in the sunshine, I leaned against the house and watched the road.

The first vehicle up the hill was Andrew's truck, pulling a flat-bed of baled hay. Martin sat in the cab with Andrew. They stopped beside the house.

"Get us some water." Andrew left the engine running and the truck door open. He shoved an empty thermos at me.

I clutched the thermos to my stomach. "The bear was here."

Andrew stopped and frowned at me.

"I shot at it but I missed. It ran off."

"Figures. The pigs all right?"

"No. The bear got two before I saw it. Ruth's okay."

"Who's Ruth?"

"One of the pigs." Why couldn't I get out what I wanted to tell him?

"I don't suppose you cleaned up the mess?"

I shook my head.

He turned back to the truck. Martin climbed out of the passenger side.

"And Joe Stone's dead."

Andrew whipped his head around.

"In his barn. Someone shot him."

Martin looked so white I thought he was going to faint.

"When?" Andrew barked at me.

"I found him about a half-hour ago." Both Martin and Andrew stared. "The police are coming."

"Hah!" Andrew went back to the truck and moved the load of hay off to the barn.

As a substitute for a mother or a father or even a friend, he was lousy.

The police came as Andrew and Martin returned from the barn and joined us by the back porch. I told Corporal Ron Ferrier what I'd found, and why I had been there.

"Why did you run out of staples?" Andrew snapped at me.

"Because I kept losing them in the grass."

"Why go to Joe Stone's place?" The corporal had his notebook out and was writing down all my answers.

"I was looking for staples," I said again.

"Funny place to look for staples." The corporal's voice was friendly but his question made me suddenly suspicious. Did he think that I had killed Joe Stone? Using Andrew's gun maybe?

I glanced back into the porch for a second, looking for the rifle. I could see it through the open door, leaning against the wall.

The corporal leaned inside the porch. He picked up the rifle, careful not to touch the area around the trigger.

"Is this yours?"

I shook my head. "Andrew's."

"And did you fire it?"

I nodded. Should I be answering these questions? Should I have a lawyer?

"Now," Corporal Ferrier said quietly, "suppose you tell me why you fired it."

"The bear," I blurted out. "To scare the bear."

"Hey," Andrew interrupted. "There were two dead pigs in the pen when I came back. There's plenty of bear sign around here. If she hadn't scared the bear away, it would have been here eating off the third pig. Now leave the girl alone. You can see she worked on that fence this morning." He pointed toward the near meadow. "And you can see she didn't finish it. That's enough questions. She has work to do here."

Corporal Ferrier raised his eyebrows, but I thought Andrew was doing fine.

The corporal looked down at me. "We'll just take this gun into the lab for a once-over."

"Aye, you can take it, but you'll be giving me a receipt for it. I might never get it back from that government office if I don't have proof that you took it."

"I'll give you a receipt." Corporal Ferrier frowned but he said nothing that wasn't polite.

"We'll want Miss George down at the station to answer some questions tomorrow."

"No you don't!" Andrew stared up at the corporal and took a step toward him. "This girl is working for me and she's wasted enough time already today. You got questions to ask her, you can come here to the ranch and ask. And you can ask them in front of me too, because that righteous, pig-headed son of mine will be up here on the next plane if I let you anywhere near this girl without me or some lawyer around."

The corporal looked down at Andrew and suddenly smiled. "Oh, take it easy, Andrew."

"Oh, ahh." Andrew wasn't backing down. "I might be giving you the same advice."

"Okay." Ferrier walked toward his cruiser.

I thought about getting a lawyer. I'd never had a lawyer for anything. Why would I need a lawyer? I'd just walked into the barn and found Joe. I hadn't put him there. But innocent people need lawyers sometimes—to prove they are innocent. I read the papers. I didn't have the money for a lawyer though, and I didn't know any in the Cariboo. Anyway, Andrew was doing just fine with the police.

The corporal nodded and folded his long legs into the cruiser. "All right. We'll come back here."

We watched the red lights disappear around the corner toward Joe's place.

"Thanks, Andrew."

"There's more staples in a bag under the bench in the barn. I'll show you. You can get on with the fence."

He stomped toward the barn and I followed, watching his thin, bony shoulders lead his body in a stumping march. Maybe he did have something good under that miserable manner.

"When you finish the fence, you can help Martin with the sheep. We're going to need some sortin' before morning."

He didn't turn around and I nodded to his back.

So that was that. If I was going to be suspected of murder, he'd help me. That didn't mean he liked me.

CHAPTER FIVE

I finished the fencing while Andrew and Martin unloaded the hay bales. The trouble with farm work is that it gives you a lot of time to think. While I pulled the wire and pounded the staples, I formed pictures in my mind: the bench in Joe's barn, the piles of machinery parts, the dust, the radios, the cans of bolts and Joe lying dead in the corner. I tried not to think about him. I never wanted to think about him again.

But I did think about myself. Just how much trouble was I in? No one in this community really knew me. Andrew defended me in front of the corporal, but how long would he do that? Maybe he only wanted to keep me working. Maybe the police wanted to accuse an outsider. I was grinding my teeth again.

Andrew left in the truck. I put the fencing tools back in the barn. Martin cleared the dirt from the gates so that they swung easily, and waited for me to get in position to sort the sheep. Andrew kept some Dorset ewes that were ready to lamb, and he wanted them separate from the others so that we could feed them differently.

"I'll use the dog and push the sheep from the meadow into the barn pen and from there into these separate ones. You work the gate." Martin waited for the dog, Lass.

I nodded. I knew how to move the gate back and forth so that one sheep would go into one pen and the next sheep into another.

"How can I tell which sheep goes into which pen?"

"I'm going to put the pregnant ones into this pen"—he pointed to my right—"and the sheep that aren't pregnant into this one." He pointed to the left.

I was patient. "Yes, but how do I tell which ones are pregnant?"

"Oh. They're lumpy and pretty wide. If you make a mistake, we'll get the strays out later."

It was quiet after Martin left with the dog. I used to like the barn—the rich, dusty smell, the windows coated in dirt, hay stacked in the loft, bits of straw on the floor. It used to seem warm and comfortable. Today it was scary, as if the dark corners held horrible secrets and I only had to look to find them. I would not think about Joe Stone's barn. This was Andrew's barn. I fought my fears alone, waiting for the sheep, and soon the bleating got louder. Then the sheep were crowding the barn pen and moving into the passageway toward me.

I had to concentrate on each sheep before it reached me so that I would have the gate open to the correct pen. Was it pregnant? Bigger than usual? Which pen should it go in? I didn't have any time or energy to think about Joe Stone. The dust was thick, and I coughed and choked but stayed working at the gate. The sheep kept coming, and they had to move on fast because more sheep were coming behind them. I looked, judged and swung the gate on about two hundred sheep. Finally the flood stopped. Thirty pregnant ewes circled in a white wool pool.

"I'll move the rest back to the meadow." Martin whistled for Lass. "Then I'll come back and help you delouse and put tags on these pregnant ones. The stuff is in the back porch on the bench. Get it, okay?"

"What am I looking for?"

"A cardboard package of louse powder and the silver punch for the ear tags. You'd better bring the yellow plastic ear tags and a felt pen."

"It's all there?"

He nodded and hurried after the sheep.

The fresh air felt wonderful. I blew the dirt from my nose and shook my hair. I was going to need a shower pretty badly. Funny about Martin. He was different today. When he worked with the sheep he seemed older, more confident. He stood up straight and gave direct orders. Not like the guy I met at Evelyn's. There he hardly spoke to me.

We worked side by side in the sheep pen all afternoon. I put numbers on the ear tags and handed them to Martin. He clamped them on the ears of the sheep that had lost their tags. They all had metal tags in one ear, but you couldn't read those from a distance, so we tagged them with a yellow plastic tag. Martin read out the number on the metal tag; I looked it up in the record book and made a replacement number for the yellow tag. It took about five minutes a sheep, so we were there a long time. While I was looking up the records, Martin shook louse powder over the back of the ewe.

We headed for the house about five. I got a drink of water and Martin collected his packsack. Because Andrew had picked him up in the hay truck, he didn't have his bike and was going to walk home; there wasn't room for anyone his man-size-medium on my bike.

"Hey, I like that tape." I could see the corner of a tape sticking out of his packsack, and I knew from the colors that it was the latest release by a rock group that was making it on the charts.

"Could I borrow that, Martin? I could listen to it on the way home."

"No!" He glared at me, grabbed his pack

and disappeared out the door.

I'd been putting the glass on the counter and my hand froze in mid-air. What was that about? We'd worked together all afternoon without any problems. What had I said? I'd just asked to borrow a tape. Why would Martin shout at me like that?

I drove home to Evelyn's slowly. Bears. Dead bodies. People yelling at me. I wasn't anxious for more trouble.

But it was quiet at the Lees'. Evelyn wanted to know all about Joe and the bear. I told her what I knew. It was comforting to sit in her kitchen, eat her homemade buns and talk about the day. It seemed a safe place to be.

The phone rang when I was buttering my third bun. Evelyn answered it, then looked over at me.

"Yes, she's here." She raised her eyebrows. "I'll tell her. Don't you give her a bad time . . . . Well, see that you don't."

"Andrew?"

"Supper."

"Oh, no!" I'd forgotten all about making his supper. "Hey, Evelyn, I've worked hard today. It's been the world's worst day. I want to have a shower. I want to wash my hair. I want to eat. I don't want to go back there."

Martin walked into the kitchen. Evelyn moved away from the sink so he could splash water on his face and wash his hands.

"What's the problem?"

"I forgot Andrew's supper."

"Tough on Andrew." He took two buns from the counter and buttered them.

"Take some buns, Susan. Andrew likes my buns." Evelyn rescued a pot from the stove. "Give the man an omelette, the buns and these cupcakes. He'll be all right."

"I'll drive you over on my bike," Martin offered. His bike was a lot bigger than mine. Now he was friendly.

I glanced at him. "That's nice of you, Martin, but I like driving and I've got lights. I'll take mine."

"Don't you let him keep you long, now. I have dinner for you here. I'll come and get you if that slave-driver keeps you more than an hour."

I smiled at her. "Don't do that. I'll be okay. But thanks, Evelyn."

Nice to have someone on my side. How could I have forgotten Andrew's supper? Easily, I thought glumly as I shrugged my packsack onto my back. I was worrying about death and didn't have time for silly things like supper.

I kicked the starter and got it on the second try.

Riding at night seems safer somehow because I can see the lights of cars and have lots of warning to get out of the way.

I was barely out of sight of the house when I saw the twin headlights of a car coming toward me. They were coming fast—far too fast for this road. I veered to the edge giving the driver lots of room, but he switched his headlights on high and accelerated—straight at me. I yanked my handlebars to the right, tried to peer into the bushes at the edge of the road and finally, when I had no more time before impact, turned the throttle on as far as I could and plunged into the woods.

As soon as the branches whipped my face, I released the throttle and grabbed the brakes. The front tire stopped moving and the back tire slued around in a circle. I flew off the seat, crashed into a willow bush and rolled into the dirt. I lay there in the dark, unbelieving for a second. I could hear the engine of my bike putt-putting quietly, and above that the sound of a car coming down the road. The same car? Maybe the driver was looking for me.

I scrambled through the bushes to my bike, turned off the lights and shut off the engine. I stared through the screen of willows. The car came slowly along the edge of the road, its headlights picking up the gravel in front of it. It would be easy to see where I'd skidded. He'd find my tire tracks quickly. My helmet! It glowed in the dark like a beacon. I ripped it off and stuffed it under my shirt.

Where could I run? It was then I realized that I hadn't broken any bones. I had a scrape on my leg and one on my cheek, but all my joints worked.

The car stopped. Someone got out and

stood looking into the bushes toward me. He might not see me if I stayed still. But if he had a flashlight, he could follow the signs of the crash and find me. Maybe I should move.

Then the lights of another car shone in the distance. The driver got back into his car and moved off. He was a long way down the road by the time the second car passed my hiding place.

I had to get out of there. I righted my bike and pushed it out of the bushes and onto the road. If that car came back, I'd hit the bushes again and hope I lived through it twice. I couldn't get anywhere going through the trees in the dark, and I was only minutes from Andrew's place. What if that car was parked in the bushes waiting for me to come by? Maybe I could make it to Andrew's.

The motor responded and I took the road faster than I'd ever done before.

"About time," Andrew said at the door. "What happened to your face?"

"I had a spill on my bike."

"Gussie's here for supper, and there isn't any."

Gussie Tetheridge was the Spiro Equipment dealer in town.

"Sorry." I took off my backpack and laid it on the counter. The zipper worked. I fished out four mashed cupcakes and some flattened buns. Then I noticed that my hands were shaking, and suddenly my legs were liquid at the knees.

CHAPTER SIX

I sat down suddenly.

Andrew eyed the remains of his meal.

"What kind of a supper is that?"

That was too much. Just too much. I was on my feet and shouting at him before I even knew what I was going to say.

"Supper? Why should I even think about supper? You self-centered egotist. I've been scared to death by a bear, to say nothing of the pigs, just about demented by finding Joe Stone's body, and you want to know where your supper is. It isn't, that's where it is. It isn't!"

Andrew drew himself up to his full height—just slightly above me—and glared. "What kind of a girlfriend is my son foisting off on me? First you're no good with a gun, then you wander around getting into barns you have no business being in, and then you don't even get all your work done."

"If Allan gives the least hint of turning out like you, I'll drop him like a hot coal!"

"If he has any sense, he'll make sure you can work before he gets serious about you."

"You don't want a hired hand around here. You want a slave! Someone with no feelings and no imagination."

"That's right. That's what I do want. And someone who can get supper ready on time."

"Now, now." Gussie tried to intervene, but neither of us paid any attention to him.

"You're lucky to get me here. Half the women in this country would be home crying their eyes out, and most of the men too. I got run off the road tonight. You know that? Someone in a car tried to run me down. I almost got killed, and you want to know where your supper is. It just isn't very important right now."

"It's important to me!"

"Susan, are you all right?" Gussie spoke with concern.

"Yes," I said shortly and turned back to Andrew. "But you're no help to me."

"I got the corporal off your back."

"Good. You did something right."

"Sit down, girl"—he was gruff and as dictatorial as usual—"and I'll fry up some eggs. Can we eat these buns?"

I shrugged. "They didn't get dirty, just mashed."

Gussie fussed over me, made tea and brought me a cup. Andrew fried the eggs and

Gussie put the knives and forks on the table.

"Ignore Andrew," Gussie said, "and tell me about the car." Gussie was a short man, even shorter than Andrew, and round. He looked like the baby angels in the old nursery rhyme books—round face, smooth, bald head and almost always a cheerful smile. He was important to the ranchers because he could keep their haying operations going by supplying spare parts quickly or slow them down by back ordering parts. He was a nice guy—easy-going and friendly. He was kind too, and right now I wanted sympathy.

"Where did the accident happen?"

I told him about the car forcing me off the road.

"Did you recognize the car or the driver?"

"No." I felt incompetent again. Why hadn't I looked for some kind of identifying information? "The driver never stood in the light, and I was pretty shaken and I didn't even try to see who it was. I just didn't want him to see me."

"But it *was* a man?" Gussie was asking me all the questions. Andrew stood at the stove and fried bacon and eggs. He was listening though. I could tell by the way he moved slowly and quietly.

"I think it was a man. I'm not sure why I think so, though."

"Here." Andrew put a plate of bacon and eggs in front of me. I thought of Evelyn's good stew and homemade buns. But a peace offering is a peace offering. I ate it. We were just drowning the last of the bacon with tea when we heard a car in the driveway.

Andrew went to the door.

"Police."

I felt my stomach muscles tighten. I was going to be sick. I took a couple of deep breaths and forced my muscles to relax, and the nausea passed. I wished I was home at Evelyn's place, in bed asleep.

Gussie was comforting. "They're not coming to see you, Susan. They are surely coming to see Andrew."

I nodded, grateful for his understanding.

Andrew jerked his head toward the stove as Ron Ferrier came into the kitchen. "Want some supper?"

"No, thanks." Ferrier took off his service hat and laid it on the counter. "I just ate."

"Tea?"

"Okay."

He pulled a chair up to the table and sat down. I stared at the bits of yellow yolk at the edge of my plate. What now?

"We didn't send the rifle off to the forensic lab." Ron Ferrier glanced at me but spoke to Andrew. "Joe Stone was killed with a shotgun. We aren't really interested in the rifle. I'll have it back to you tomorrow."

Andrew plopped the teapot down in front of Ferrier. "You can stop suspecting Susan of murder then."

"Everyone is a suspect in a violent death.

Even you."

"Hah!" Andrew snorted. "Haven't liked that miserable Joe Stone for years. No one has. But no one killed him before this. Why would anyone around here kill him now? He was no more miserable now than he'd always been."

Ferrier stirred sugar into his tea. "There were a number of stolen radios, small televisions and electrical appliances—irons, hair curlers, things like that—sitting on the bench where Joe was killed. He was filing off the serial numbers."

"Oh, ahh, that so?" Andrew tossed back the last of his cooled tea.

"Yes," Ferrier said. "He was a fence for stolen goods, as far as we can tell."

"Good old Joe," Andrew said. "He never did want honest work."

"So what are you looking for now?" Gussie asked that.

"We're looking for any sign of a connection between Joe and other people in this community. I know, Andrew, someone from outside this community could be dealing with Joe, but we'll look here first." He turned to me.

"Did you have any dealings with Joe Stone yourself, Miss George?"

"No." I pushed my plate away. "Well, once he came over here and asked to borrow Andrew's compressor. I let him into the truck garage to use it. And I saw him once at Fred and Evelyn's place. He was borrowing something there too." I searched my memory. "That's all, I guess."

"Did you ever visit him at his place?"

"No."

"So this morning was the first time you'd gone there?"

It seemed days ago, but it was only this morning. "Yes."

"And you just went into the barn?"

I was silent for a moment. The truth was going to get me into more trouble.

"No. I poked my head into his house."

"Why did you do that?"

"To see if he was home."

"Why would you expect him to be in the house?"

I caught my bottom lip in my teeth. It didn't seem to me that any answer was going to be right. I looked at Andrew.

"Why not?" he said. "You'll have a hard time pinning anything on this girl. For one thing, she isn't used to guns and probably wouldn't know how to come even close to hitting Joe."

"Anyone can connect with a shotgun."

Andrew ignored him. "And for another, you have to have some kind of evidence and you don't have any. So turn your attention to the person who wants to kill her, why don't you?"

Corporal Ferrier looked surprised. "What's been going on?"

I told him about the car and showed the scrapes on my face.

He wrote the information down in his notebook. "Any witnesses?"

I shook my head and looked at Andrew again. No one was going to believe me. The police might think I'd fallen off my bike and made up the whole story. I'd had enough.

"I'm going home."

Gussie jumped to his feet. "I'll take you, Susan. You've had a hard day."

"Thanks, Gussie, but I've got my bike."

"I'll put it in the back of my pickup."

"I'll escort her home." Corporal Ferrier stood up and reached for his hat. "You can ride your bike," he told me. "I'll follow and see that you get to the Lees' ranch."

It was more an order than an invitation. The corporal wanted to make sure that I went straight home.

"You don't know anything about the stolen goods, Andrew? Or you, Gussie?"

Both men shook their heads.

"All right then." He nodded his goodbyes.

The headlights from the police car lit the road in front and beside me. I was careful to follow all the driving rules, and hoped that I wasn't doing anything wrong. But I still had time to think. Andrew had helped me a little there at the house, but it seemed to me that if the police were looking at me as a suspect, a murder suspect, I'd better help myself.

The police car left me at the driveway, and

I wheeled into the yard. I was dirty, tired and misunderstood. I wanted a hot bath and a safe bed. I leaned my bike against the house and slipped in the back door.

The Lees were watching television when I walked through the kitchen. I called a hello but went straight to the bathroom. Twenty minutes in hot water was wonderful. I washed my hair, put on my warm pyjamas and curled up in my bed. Was I safe here? I thought of the dogs sleeping on the porch and around the barn. They barked if a stranger came into the yard. That would have to be good enough.

CHAPTER SEVEN

When I woke in the morning, my legs felt Krazy-glued at the knees. I'd slept on damp hair, and the only way I could control the wild look was to braid it into one thick braid down my back. That would be cool later in the afternoon. The trouble was that braiding my hair pulled it away from my face and left that ugly red scrape exposed on my cheek. I looked at myself in the mirror and shrugged. The ugly look.

Martin had breakfast with Andrew and settled the day's work for both of us. We had to feed the pregnant ewes and clean out the pens.

I met him in the sheep barn where he was throwing alfalfa pellets into the ewes' pens. When he finished, we put the feed buckets back into the bins and took shovels from the wall. The pens had wooden floors and were easy to clean—if we did it often. It wasn't my favorite chore, but it was a great fitness exercise, especially for the arm muscles. I started at one end, Martin at the other, shoveling dirt and manure into a cart that we would later haul outside and dump. Martin worked quickly. With his muscles, lifting the shovelfuls of dirt was no problem. I worked more slowly, but I did make a difference—the pens were clean behind me. That rhythmic thrust, lift, throw, thrust, lift, throw set up a relaxed physical trance that let my mind bubble along with stray thoughts. I thought about Martin. Today he was friendly—at least as friendly as he ever was. Had been last night too when he offered to drive me to Andrew's. That wasn't like Martin. Was he hoping I'd forget the way he'd blown up at me? Why had he blown up at me? Didn't seem to be personal. And if it wasn't personal, was there something wrong with that tape I'd wanted to hear?

We took a break in the sunshine after we dumped our second load. Andrew had dug a section of the hillside away so that all the manure and compost could be dumped into a pit. He left it there to decompose until he thought it was ripe enough to drive into with his front-end loader and haul away for fertilizer. We sat well back from the edge of the pit and took deep breaths of fresh air.

"Hey, Martin?"

"Uh huh."

"What was the matter with that tape I

wanted to borrow yesterday?" Maybe the best way to find out was to ask.

Martin said nothing; he just looked away over the meadow into the trees beyond.

"Was it stolen?" I persisted. "Are you in trouble with stolen tapes?"

I could see the muscles in his arms tighten and his hands clench.

"So what? Lotsa kids have stolen tapes."

"Your mother'll die."

"My mother knows all about it."

"She does?" I didn't think Evelyn would approve of stealing tapes. "Come on. How about your dad?"

"My dad hates my guts. I wouldn't tell him anything."

"What happened?"

Martin picked up a handful of stones and tossed them one at a time over the edge into the pit.

"I got caught lifting some tapes at the music store in town. The cops took me in, and my mom had to come down and sign me out."

"When was this?"

"Three months ago."

"And . . . what happened?"

"Nothing, really. I had to do some community work at the store. My mom . . . well . . . my mom was upset."

"And your dad?"

"We didn't tell my dad. He hates me anyway. He'd give me a bad time, but he'd give Mom a worse one if he knew."

"Why were you so upset when I spotted the tape? I couldn't know it was stolen."

"That one wasn't stolen. I guess I thought . . . I don't know. The police were hanging around you, and I guess I thought they might think of me when they found all those stolen radios and things in Joe's barn. I don't know why I got sore." He shrugged.

"Was it the first time you'd stolen anything?"

Martin was quiet. He looked at me out of the corner of his eye for a moment and picked up the cart.

"Hey, wait a minute, Martin. You're not stupid. You're not going to get panicky over one tape. Why are you so afraid of the police? What are you up to?"

"Nothing! Get off my back!"

"Okay! Okay!"

We finished cleaning the barn and put the cart back. It wasn't until Martin was down at the small-acre field opening the gate for the ewes that I wondered how he had known about the stolen radios in Joe's barn before the police told us.

Right then I heard a truck rattle over the cattleguard and watched Gussie Tetheridge park by the house.

I met him at the corner of the barn. "Hi, Gussie."

"Hello, Susan. Feeling better today?"

"Yeah. Thanks."

"All alone?" He smiled.

"No, Martin's here. Did you want something?"

"I wanted to tell Andrew that the wheel bearing he's looking for will be in on the bus tonight. Could you let him know?"

"Sure."

Martin came around the corner and almost bumped into Gussie. He started, then turned around and left. He hadn't said a word.

Gussie and I stared after him.

"Good heavens!" Gussie raised his eyebrows. "What's the matter with Martin?"

"I don't know. He's touchy. He needs a friend, I guess."

"You?"

I considered it. "Maybe."

Gussie looked at me seriously for a moment. "That's good of you, Susan. But perhaps Martin won't confide in you."

"Maybe not." I shrugged. "I'll give Andrew your message, Gussie. I'd better get back to work."

He waved and left in his pickup. I joined Martin on the other side of the barn. He had six portable fences flat on the ground and was repairing broken boards. I found a hammer and some nails and started on the fence closest to me.

I didn't say anything to Martin. If he was so upset that he wouldn't even talk to Gussie—Gussie who was so friendly and inoffensive—then he was in some trouble. If he wanted to tell me, he would. If he couldn't tell me, there was no use asking him any questions.

We'd finished three of the fences when we heard a motorbike on the other side of the barn. As we straightened and turned to look, a big Yamaha 200 pulled in. The driver stood, kicked out the stand and shut off the motor. He swung his leg over the bike, then pulled off his helmet.

"How ya doing, Martin?"

"Get lost."

"Is that a nice way to talk to a buddy?"

Suddenly everything was still. I could hear the small sounds of chickens cackling in the loft and the sheep bleating in the small-acre pasture. They sounded loud against the silence of the yard.

"I told you, Paul. Don't come here. Andrew won't like it."

"He's in the hay fields. He won't be back for hours. I want to talk to you. Who's this?"

"Nobody you know."

"She must be the new girl staying at your place. Susan, right?"

He moved a couple of steps toward me and—I couldn't help it—I backed away. He looked like a million other kids I knew: as tall as Martin but skinny; blond hair; blue eyes; a T-shirt that said "Angel Face;" jeans. Nothing different, nothing really special. Except for the knife at his belt.

"You're the one that found Joe Stone. You kill him? I'd like to have killed him myself a couple of times. Did Martin here let you in on a good deal? You shouldn't have done that, Martin."

Martin moved closer to me. "I didn't. I'm not part of the gang anymore. I told you that."

"Yeah, you told me. But it looks like you let our little friend in on it. What would she be doing in Joe Stone's barn if she wasn't after good prices or money?"

"I was after staples."

Paul looked puzzled for a moment. "Staples? What the . . . ? Staples? Look, the cops won't believe that. No one would believe that. You'd better think of somethin' better than that. Joe wasn't into that kind of fencing." He laughed and then shoved his face closer to mine. "I'm warning you. Don't mess with our operation. We got a good thing going here. Someone else will work for us. We'll be back in business real soon. Don't mess with us or someone will mess with you. It might even be me." He fingered the knife on his belt.

I told myself that he was only a kid, a bully, but I was backed against the barn wall by then and not feeling brave. Martin moved closer, his fists clenched. We were in trouble. I reached out with my hand and connected with the pitchfork. This guy was crazy.

"Okay, girl?" he said and picked the knife

from his belt.

"Ayaah!" I lunged, screamed and shoved the pitchfork at him. He jumped back and dropped the knife.

Martin was beside me swinging the hammer over his head. "Out, Paul! Go!" Paul hesitated a moment, but I had the pitchfork high and Martin was ready to attack. "Get out of here! Don't come back and don't come anywhere near Susan. I'll tell the police."

"You tell the police, and I'll tell them everything you've been involved in, you traitor. You'll sink with me, Mart, don't think you won't."

Paul snatched the knife and put it back in his belt, turned his back and marched over to his bike.

"Get to the barn door, Susan." Martin's voice was urgent. I didn't think. I did just as he said and sidled along the wall to the door.

Paul switched on the bike, kicked it into gear and gunned the engine. He swung the bike in a circle and ran it at us like a charging ram. We sidestepped into the barn. He missed us, cursed at the air and roared out of the yard.

I dropped the pitchfork. "Uh, I don't like your friends much, Martin. A little . . . uh, pushy, don't you think?"

Martin leaned against the doorway and stared after Paul. "I don't see any way out of this mess."

"You want to tell me about it?"

"You don't want to know."

"I'm asking."

He slammed his fist against the barn wall. "No! Leave me alone, Susan. Just leave me alone!"

I didn't know what to do, so I stood there, saying nothing.

He turned, picked up a wrench and walked over to the tractor. I went into the house to put Andrew's supper in the oven. Martin was in deep trouble for sure. He'd been in some kind of gang dealing in stolen property and now wanted out of it. I could see that pretty clearly. But did that gang deal in murder? How much of what I knew should I tell the police? Any of it? Martin could be in worse trouble if I told anyone anything.

I shut the oven door with a snap. Why didn't they teach you more practical stuff in school? Math, English, Social Studies—what good were they in a situation like this? How was I supposed to decide whether to keep quiet or talk?

I tried Martin one more time before we left for the day.

"Will that creep come back here one day when I'm alone?"

"Andrew said you weren't to be left alone anymore."

"Oh." Andrew must have believed me last night. I was so surprised I didn't say another word.

CHAPTER EIGHT

You'd think that after Joe's murder and Paul's threats, something would have happened in the next week, but nothing did. I worked hard at the ranch and got blisters on my palms from the barn shovel. My mom phoned to tell me that my brother Joe was engaged. That was great. His girlfriend Julie was right for him. My younger brother, Luke, had broken his arm trying to hang glide. That sounded like him. Otherwise they were all okay. I missed them a little, but I wasn't ready to go home yet.

The weather held fine and the men continued with the haying. Martin helped me on the ranch, sometimes going out to the hay fields to help bring in a load.

Evelyn and I had deep discussions about Life and Men and the Future. She married young; before she'd had a chance to really decide what to do with her life—zap—she was a wife and mother. I didn't know what I wanted. I missed Allan a little, but when I was busy, I didn't think about him at all.

Evelyn thought that I had great opportunities. "You could be a truck driver or a doctor or a real estate salesman. Just about anything!"

"I don't want to be a real estate sales anything. My mom sold real estate for a year when I was ten. We all had to help with the signs, the telephone messages, the Sunday open houses. We hated it."

"What do you want?"

"I want to be a pilot."

"That'll do. How do you do that?"

"First I have to get a private pilot's license, then I go to commercial pilot's school, and then I get a flying job and flying experience."

"We have an outfit at the airport that teaches flying. Why don't you take lessons while you're here? I'll join you. We can take lessons together."

I blinked. When she got an idea, she really rolled with it. There wasn't any reason why she couldn't take flying lessons. She just needed a ground school course and a good medical. But she was old, more than forty! For some reason, it didn't seem right. Then I juggled pictures in my mind, moving Evelyn from her kitchen where she always worked to the cockpit of a plane.

"Sure," I said. "Let's do it." If she could do it, I could do it.

We started ground school two nights a week, learning all about weather and radios and aerodynamics. It helped to have Evelyn with me for those classes. For one thing, she drove us there in her truck, and for another, we talked about the classes all the way home. That helped me to remember the material. We got to know each other pretty well too. It was great to have a friend. Funny, I had to get away from Allan and my family so I could be sure that I was independent, and then I worked really hard at making a friend so I wouldn't be alone.

The third lesson was on weather, so that night we talked about fronts, nimbus clouds and thunderheads most of the way home. The headlights on Evelyn's truck picked up the dips and bumps in the gravel road.

"The police were at the house today."

"Did they want me?" I hadn't seen the police for two weeks. I thought they'd crossed me off their list; I hoped they'd crossed me off their list.

"No, they wanted Martin."

"Oh-oh."

"They just wanted to know when he'd seen Joe Stone last. Martin didn't kill Joe Stone, Susan. Martin's had his troubles but he's a good boy. He's loyal and compassionate and fine. He had a small brush with the law a few months ago, but he hasn't been in any trouble since and I don't want him in any trouble."

I stared at her. I wasn't planning on getting Martin into any trouble.

"I don't want you accused of murdering Joe Stone, Susan, but I won't stand by and have you cleared only to have Martin accused."

"Well, no. Of course not."

"So," Evelyn took a deep breath, "so don't do anything that would point the police in Martin's direction. I won't have it. You understand? I won't have it."

I was shocked speechless for a moment. I realized that Evelyn would lie to help Martin. And now she seemed to be asking me to do the same. Would she throw me to the police to save him? I felt anger begin low in my stomach and start to rise. But I had a sudden thought. My mother would do the same for me. She'd feel compelled to defend me. That's what Evelyn was doing. Maybe someday that's what I'd do for my child. The "she-bear" complex or something.

"I understand, Ev."

"It's not that I don't like you, Susan. You know that."

"I know that."

"But . . ."

"But I'm not your child."

"That's right."

"It's okay." I understood all right, but I was hurt too.

Evelyn turned the truck down the driveway. "Are you having any lambs over at

Andrew's place these days?"

"They should start coming this week."

"It'll be busy then."

I nodded. "So they tell me."

Evelyn parked in the yard and shut off the motor. "You'll find out," she said. "Lambing can be hectic."

She was right.

The lambs started coming the next day, and I was frantically trying to match ewes with their lambs so that they would pay attention to the little ones and let them nurse. Martin and I put portable fences around the new pairs, and I fed them pellets and water and tried to see that all was well.

The weatherman was predicting a rainstorm, so Andrew was anxious to get the last of the hay in. Naturally, that was the day one of the tractors broke down. Andrew parked it in the yard and told me to expect Gussie out to work on it. He needed Martin in the field to try to get more hay loaded with less equipment, so I was on my own. I was feeding and watching the sheep and trying to do all the other chores when I spotted one of the ewes lying in the yard huffing and panting.

She'd been lying there all morning, but I hadn't thought about her much until about eleven o'clock when I realized that she hadn't moved. I walked over to her.

"What's the matter, old girl?"

I walked behind her and peered at her

backside. I could see the smooth, wet tip of the black head of a lamb ready to be born.

"Can't you push that out?" I'd studied Andrew's lambing books, so I knew this was no simple birth. If it had been, the ewe wouldn't have been trying to push the lamb out all morning.

I found a lambing book on the porch and studied the diagrams that showed all the difficult births. Twins could be so tangled up in each other that they couldn't be born until you straightened out all the legs. Lambs could try to come out backwards or crossways.

"I'll try to help you, old girl, but I don't know if I'm going to be any good at it."

I got a bucket of warm water and some dish detergent. I brought the textbook out with me, opened it to the page with the diagrams on it and propped it up on a bale of hay. I dragged another bale closer to the poor ewe and then, using all the strength I had, hauled her against it until she was propped with her back feet higher than her stomach. I washed my hands, left them wet and squirted soap on them for cleanliness and lubrication.

The little dark, wet head was still there. I carefully eased my fingers in around it then pushed it back until I could slide my hand down the body of the lamb.

The sheep rolled her eyes at me but didn't struggle. I peered past her at the book spread out on the hay bale. The diagrams looked so clear, but I wasn't sure which of the bumps and bones I was feeling belonged to what part of the lamb.

I wanted two front feet and a head to come out together. I found one front foot and followed it along the body of the lamb until I felt the head, then down the other side to the other foot. That was all right: two front feet and a head. But there was another foot there. Three front feet and a head? Was this a freak?

"Susan, you nut." It was two lambs, naturally—four front feet. I found the third foot and slowly pushed it back. Then I grasped the two front feet and pulled gently down toward the ground. The ewe groaned and pushed, and the lamb's head and front feet slipped out.

"Good girl!" I looked at the mother. She rolled her eyes at me again and pushed. I pulled the bale of hay away, and the ewe's backside eased onto the ground. She pushed again, and the lamb slid right out.

It looked dead: wet, dark, no life at all. "Come on, sweetie, breathe."

It shuddered, then lay still. I held my breath. What did I do now?

It shuddered again, coughed and lay still. Then it sneezed and started to breathe.

I turned back to the mother. "You have another one, old lady, come on."

But the mother paid no attention to me. She was on her feet and nuzzling her baby. I stepped back. Maybe twins don't have to be born one right after the other. The mother licked her baby's head and nose. That was smart. She'd get all that guck away from the breathing passages. I didn't think sheep had much in the way of brains, but this one was doing the sensible thing. The lamb shook its head and gave a soft little bleat. The mother shoved it with her nose, and it struggled to its feet. I watched fascinated—a tiny scrap tottering around its mother.

The ewe lay back down on the ground and strained until the second little head popped out and the body quickly followed. This one took a little longer to start breathing, and I was worried that it had died. But it struggled to its feet, and both wet lambs staggered around the mother's legs looking for dinner while she licked them and nuzzled them and made sure they belonged to her.

Two healthy lambs. I felt wonderful. Even Andrew would have to agree that I'd done the right thing this time.

I heard a truck approaching and looked up to see Gussie Tetheridge pull into the yard. Great! I could tell him about the lambs.

"Very well done, Susan," Gussie approved. "You've learned quite a lot since you've been here. You must feel pretty good about it."

"Thanks, Gussie, I do." I washed my hands at the back porch sink. "Are you here to work on the tractor?"

"Yes, I have the part."

"Andrew will be glad of that."

"It's going to rain."

"Before you get the tractor fixed?"

"Perhaps."

He pulled a package from the back of his truck and walked over to the tractor. I watched him move heavily across the yard. He was fat and moved awkwardly, rolling a little on his heels. Maybe being a slow walker gave him time to listen to people. Perhaps that's why he always knew everything.

"Gussie, are the police getting any further in their investigation of Joe's death?"

"I thought you might know more about that than I do, Susan." He lifted the battery out of the tractor and set it on the ground.

"Me? No. Not a thing. No one tells me anything. I just know that he was dead when I found him."

"Anything else? Anything at all about that day?"

I thought about that day, the way I'd ridden there on my bike . . . "I saw a gray car travelling down the road pretty fast. It had a local license plate with the letters SEG. I didn't get the numbers."

Gussie dropped a wrench and had to grope around in the dust for it. "SEG . . . lots of people in this area have those letters on their license plates. I do myself, on my car. What made you remember that?"

"They're my initials."

"I see. Well, I don't think that's going to be helpful. The car might not have anything to do with the murder, and there must be hundreds of cars with those letters."

I nodded. "I don't really remember anything important but I think I should try to find out as much as I can."

Gussie opened the package and took a small bolt from the papers. "You'd better be careful about where you go and what you learn. Somebody killed Joe Stone, and that somebody might well kill you."

"I'll be careful," I promised.

It seemed odd to be talking about death here in Andrew's yard. The sun was warm, Gussie was friendly, the lambs were newly born. Death seemed a long way away.

Gussie replaced the bolt inside the tractor just as a truck pulled into the yard. It was Andrew.

"Your luck's in, Gussie." I grinned at him. "You finished the tractor before Andrew got home."

He stared at me for a second, then saw Andrew's truck. "He couldn't have timed it better."

CHAPTER NINE

Judith was home. She'd done her time in the southern Cariboo, making sure that the public's health was looked after, and now she was back at McLeese Lake. I'd been curious about her. Everyone talked about her as if she was tall, aggressive and somehow unattractive. But she was short, with auburn hair and gray eyes, and beautiful. She smelled like flowers. I think that older women use more perfume than women my age.

After I'd seen her with Andrew though, I understood why people thought she was bigger than she was. She was what my mother calls a "scrapper." She stood up to Andrew, stared him in the eye and made me think of a cat we'd had once—small but a real fighter. If she could handle Andrew, she could probably handle the whole Cariboo. I liked the way she looked straight at me and smiled, as if we'd been friends in a previous life and there wasn't anything we couldn't talk about.

"Enough of all these carefully understated accusations," she told me. "You come for supper at Andrew's place. I'll cook it. And we'll show the people of this town whether you're a murderer. A murderer in the family. Nonsense!"

I didn't remind her that neither of us was actually one of the Ross family yet and that her marriage and mine might never take place. I wasn't sure I wanted to marry Allan, and I couldn't see why anyone would want to marry Andrew.

"He has his faults, I know that," she said as we set plates out on the table. Andrew was on the back porch washing the barn grime from his face. "He's pig-headed, rigid, shortsighted and penny-pinching." I nodded. "On the other hand"—she dished the potatoes into a bowl—"he's honest, loyal, protective, hard-working and fair. I can deal with the faults if he keeps those qualities."

"But, well, Judith . . ." It was a personal question that I wanted to ask and I hesitated. But Judith was easy to talk to. "Do you love him?"

Judith plopped the stew on the table and wiped her hands on her apron. "Oh yes, of course I do." She looked over the table searching for missing utensils. Then she looked at me. "Quite madly." She said the last seriously and softly. I was impressed.

Andrew talked about the price of calves at

the last stock sale and the chances of getting all the hay off. I wanted to know about the bear. Andrew told me that one of the men on a ranch to the north had shot a brown bear. It was probably my killer. "Means that bear won't be back here."

I felt relieved for a moment until Andrew added, "No reason why there shouldn't be another, of course."

I caught Judith's eye, and she laughed. "How's the rest of your life going?" She reached for the empty plates. "Are you making any headway? Finding out about the murder, I mean?" She stood and turned to stack the dirty dishes on the counter.

"Not really. I told the police everything I know. I think I did, anyway. It's hard to remember what I talked about with Evelyn and Andrew, and what I told the police. I did tell them about the license plate letters, didn't I, Andrew?"

He nodded. "So the sergeant said."

I looked at him sharply. "Have you been down at the station asking questions?"

"Seemed best. They haven't been back to bother you, have they?"

"No. And I don't have anything more to tell them except about the perfume."

"What's that?"

"I smelled perfume in Joe's house the day he died. But it could have been anything."

"What kind of perfume?"

I tried to remember exactly what kind of a

smell it had been. I remembered poking my head into Joe's house, calling, then smelling the perfume in the air.

"Lilac! Lilac perfume. Like yours, Judith. Is that lilac perfume you're wearing?"

"No, rose."

"Oh. Do you think that's important? Should I report that?"

Andrew shrugged. "I don't know. I'll tell them if you want."

"Thanks." If he was down at the station regularly, he might as well pass on the message. I wondered why he was paying so much attention to the police. Was he looking after himself? Or was he looking after me?

I'd had enough talk of the murder, so I asked Judith when her wedding was to be.

"October eighth," she said.

"September fifteenth." Andrew was just as emphatic.

"I want it in October, Andrew. That's when my sister can come."

"I want it in September so your sister can't come."

Judith raised her eyebrows and leaned forward.

"I've booked the church for the eighth of October."

"And I've booked the hall for the fifteenth of September."

They argued happily for the rest of the meal without settling anything. Neither was upset and both enjoyed it. I wondered if they'd have their party in September and their wedding in October. Probably.

Andrew left us to do the dishes and wandered into the living room to watch the football game on television.

I looked after him, and Judith shook her head.

"If you're looking for a liberated man, Susan, you're looking in the wrong direction. He's got lots of qualities, but he'll never think that washing dishes is anything but women's work. I'm not going to waste energy trying to change that."

I picked up the tea towel. She was probably wise. It would be a waste of energy.

"Dishes aren't that important to me." Well, it was her marriage. But if I ever got married, I wasn't going to start out doing all the dishes.

I passed behind her and started drying. I smelled flowers again.

"Lilac," I said. "You *are* wearing lilac."

"Yes, I am." Judith turned to look straight at me. "I was there."

I sat down on a kitchen chair. If she told me she killed Joe Stone, I was going to be sick.

"You were? At Joe's the afternoon he was murdered?"

"Well, I guess it was the afternoon he was murdered, but I didn't know that until I got back to town. I was there to see Joe . . ." She glanced toward the living room, but a roar from the football crowd reassured her that Andrew was settled for some time. "I wanted to see Joe about buying his ranch for Andrew for a wedding present."

"You could buy the ranch?" I was breathing much easier.

"I have quite a bit of money, and I want to come into this marriage as a partner not a slave. That'd be important in the years to come, I think. So I wanted to buy Joe's ranch."

"You were in the kitchen at Joe's place talking about buying the ranch?" I wiped the plate over and over, thinking about that day.

"For a few minutes. Then I walked out to my car with Joe and left him heading for the barn."

"Was there anyone around when you left?" The plate was very dry. I put it on the table.

"No one in the yard. I met Martin on the road, or at least some kid on a motorbike like Martin's, with a yellow helmet like Martin's. You know how hard it is to see faces when kids have their helmets on."

"Have you reported this to the police?"

"No." She rinsed a plate under the tap and stacked it in the dish rack. "It was only today that I realized that I had seen Joe on the day he died. I haven't decided what I ought to do with the information."

I stood and reached for a wet plate. "See anyone else?"

"No. Just a gray car on the road near here."

"License number?"

Judith shook her head. "Sorry."

"What are you going to do?"

"I guess I'll tell the police, but don't you tell Andrew."

I looked at her.

"I still want to buy the ranch and I don't want that man interfering in the sale."

"Could you run both ranches?"

Judith drained the soapy water and wiped the counter. "Oh, yes. It's just what we need. Andrew has been wanting it for years, but he wouldn't pay Joe's price."

"And you will."

"I would have. I don't know what the estate is going to ask." She rinsed the cloth and hung it over the tap.

I finished drying the last cup, tipped the rubber mat to drain the water and draped the tea towel over it. "I can't figure it out, Judith. You were there that day. Someone in a gray car may have been there. Martin may have been there. Do you think Martin . . . ?"

"I shouldn't think so." Judith sloshed lotion on her hands and offered me some. "I don't think he'd have the nerve."

She might be right. She was an experienced nurse who knew a lot about people's emotions. But as I massaged the lotion into my hands, I thought about the way Martin had faced Paul. Martin showed courage that day.

And he was desperately unhappy.

I phoned Allan later that night.

"You should come back here. I miss you and you're getting into trouble up there."

"I'm doing okay, and your dad's actually helping me."

"He'd better. Look, why don't you just come back?"

"Why?"

"So I can look after you."

"You don't think I can look after myself?" How old does he think I am?

"Damn it, Susan! Don't be an idiot."

I hung up. I didn't want to deal with a boyfriend who turned every emotion into anger. He didn't have to shout.

CHAPTER TEN

I pounded staples into fences, shoveled out barns, cooked, fed animals and did some accounts. Allan phoned once a week. He didn't shout anymore; he listened. He was in the middle of investigating a series of break-ins and couldn't get away to see me.

Every evening I ate Evelyn's wonderful food and twice a week went with her to ground school classes. Because she could go during the day when I was working, she was ahead of me and already taking flight instruction. She was so excited about flying she was almost poetic. "Gorgeous scenery," she told me one night as she trimmed the edges of a blueberry pie. "I can see our ranch and all the hills and creeks around it. The world's set out like a kid's jigsaw puzzle with roads and towns and trees spread out as far as you can see."

I smiled at her. She acted as if she'd

discovered a new world. Maybe it was like that—a new country, a new territory.

"I made Horace take me over the ranch a couple of times. It was interesting to see how we've laid the buildings out and how the trails converge at the barn." She smiled at me and licked the pie filling off a spoon. "It's exciting up there, you know, and beautiful."

She put the pie in the oven and wiped her hands on her jeans. "Funny though, some of the things you see. Today I noticed a shack in the bush between our place and Andrew's—just off the trail about halfway along."

"That back trail that comes out in Andrew's near meadow?"

Evelyn nodded. "Uh huh. I didn't even know we had a shack there. It's not a very big one—more of a lean-to than a house."

Martin drifted into the kitchen and opened the refrigerator. He poured milk into a glass and wandered over to the table.

"Dad home?"

"No, he drove the tractor over to Andrew's place, then he's going back out to the field."

"Oh." The muscles in Martin's shoulders relaxed. He leaned over the table. "What are you two talking about?"

"Flying."

"Oh, great. I'd like to do that some day."

Evelyn smiled at him, and for the first time, I saw a smile on Martin's face.

"Maybe I could ask Dad to finance lessons for you."

"Hah! Dad would just tell me that I had to learn to drive the baler properly before he'd put a dime into flying lessons."

Evelyn nodded. "Maybe so. Maybe you and I could work out something. Flying lessons traded for fourteen years of dishes or six years of garbage duty."

"I'll get lessons when I want them, Mom, don't worry. You don't have to look after me."

"You see how it is, Susan. His father has him convinced that women are not to be consulted. That's one thing they agree on." I looked at her sharply, but she was smiling.

Martin looked solemn and leaned back in his chair, mimicking Fred. "Now relax, Evelyn, and let me run my own life. You mind your kitchen and let me look after my own business."

"Listen, my little rooster, if you get much more like your father, I'm going to start nagging you."

It was good to see the two of them getting along so well, but it didn't seem right that they should make fun of Fred. He wasn't there to defend himself, and it seemed a bit mean. Maybe that was the only way to live with him. I didn't want it to be like that when I was a parent.

"When are you going to solo, Mom?"

"Maybe soon. I was flying over the ranch

this afternoon."

Martin nodded. "I heard the plane."

"Martin, do you know anything about a shed in the bush off the south trail?"

The effect on Martin was instantaneous. He turned white and stared at his mother. Evelyn didn't notice because she had turned around and picked up the phone book as she asked the question. By the time she looked up again, Martin had his eyes closed as he drank the glass of milk.

"Do you, Martin?"

"No, nothing."

"Aren't you even curious about it? I wonder who built it and why."

"Probably kids."

"Oh, that's right. You could get to it pretty easily from the McKenzie Creek Road, couldn't you? I bet kids built it and used it for a clubhouse or something."

"Probably," Martin said and stared hard at the bottom of his glass.

"I suppose I should report it to the police." She turned to pick up the phone.

I watched Martin. He looked as though he was frozen to his chair. Only his eyes followed Evelyn's movements.

I touched her arm. "Uh, why don't you wait a bit, Evelyn? Andrew checks in with Ron Ferrier all the time. I'll tell him about it."

"No trouble. I can phone."

Martin was looking at me now.

I glanced at the clock. "It's change of shift down there at the station. They'll be busy."

Evelyn looked at the time. "So it is. All right. You tell Andrew. I wonder how long it's been there."

"Years, maybe."

"No more than two. We did some brush clearing in that area two years ago. We'd have seen it then."

"I'll let you know if I find out anything."

She hesitated for a moment, the phone book in her hand, but decided to leave the shack to me.

Martin left in a hurry and I went to bed. What was Martin up to? What was going on in that shack? I wondered if Martin's old gang met there. I'd report the shack to Andrew, all right, but I'd check it over myself first.

I took the back trail to Andrew's in the morning. It was beautiful in the early sunlight—brown earth, green pine, occasionally scarlet berries in clumps low to the ground. The pine sent the smell of pitch into the air, and I could almost—but not quite—forget about the bear.

I had been watching the trail in front of me to make sure I didn't hit a rock or a stump, and I noticed that I was following a bike track. It wasn't always obvious, but now and then I saw a clump of fresh dirt lying loose on a corner and the tread marks of tires in a patch of soft earth.

The tracks turned off the trail and down an old logging road. I stopped my bike, parked it against a tree and shut it off.

I stared at the logging road. If I went down it and ran into trouble, no one would be able to help me. If I didn't go down it, I wouldn't know anything more about the shack. There wasn't much choice in that. I started down the trail. I'd be careful.

On the straight stretches I walked on the old road, but at every curve I slipped off and cut through the trees so that I could look ahead without being seen by anyone coming the opposite way.

That was smart, because at the third curve I peered through the trees and saw the shack. Martin's friend Paul stood at the door looking toward the main trail.

He must have heard my bike and then heard the motor stop. I couldn't have announced my arrival more loudly. Of course, the silence following that loud bike-engine noise would tell anyone in the woods that I was somewhere near.

Paul was alert and scanning the woods, first one side and then the other. I stayed perfectly still. Was I wearing anything bright, anything he could spot against the trees? Yes, a yellow shirt. As soon as he looked the other way, I slipped back into the trees even further.

I was not going to get into the shack with Paul standing guard over it. I wanted distance between me and that Paul. He looked bigger than he had the other day, and meaner. I dropped to my knees, crawled out onto the old road at the other side of the curve, stood up and ran for my bike.

I glanced back once. There was no one behind me. I'd taken two curves and a straight stretch before I looked back again. This time Paul was there, running hard. My bike was ahead of me, leaning against the tree. I pushed with the ball of my foot and flew toward it. Then tripped on a rock. I hit the ground with my shoulder and my knees but was on my feet in an instant. I grabbed the handlebars, pulled the bike away from the tree, turned the key and kicked the starter. Nothing happened. "Oh, no. Not now!" I groaned. I didn't look up. I figured Paul would get me soon enough. I didn't want to know where he was. I kicked it again. This time it started. I pushed off—then looked for Paul. He had stopped at the main trail. I had no speed. He could still get me. But he stayed where he was. I turned the bike, gave it power and flew down the trail.

He had a bike. He might come after me.

I didn't look back all the way to Andrew's place. I concentrated on the trail ahead. It took a lot of attention and skill to keep the bike on the road. I took the corners so low that my jeans dusted the ground, and all the time I felt as though Paul was just behind me. But I pulled into Andrew's yard without him.

Close. That was too close.

Gussie was under the tractor and crawled out when he heard my bike.

I shut the motor off and left the bike by the barn. I wanted it handy today.

"Morning, Susan."

"Hi, Gussie. What happened to Andrew's tractor?"

"It's Fred's tractor, Susan, and it's having electrical problems. Andrew has the tools I need so they left it here for me. How are things with you?"

I swallowed and then told him about the shack and about Paul.

"Is Martin mixed up in this, do you think?" Gussie watched my face and then squatted down by the tools he'd laid out on the ground and picked up a big crescent wrench.

I leaned against the barn and tried to think things out.

"Martin has some kind of problem. He was upset when Evelyn mentioned the shack. He might have been mixed up in some stealing in the past, but I don't think he is now. I think that Paul is though. And Joe was right in the middle."

"You've got quite a lot figured out, Susan." Gussie spoke as though he thought I had brains. He made me feel smart.

"Thanks, Gussie, but I don't suppose I know any more than the police do."

"Oh, I think you do."

"Really?"

The sun glinted silver off the crescent wrench as Gussie swung it back and forth. "I don't think the police have put together Paul and Joe and the shack."

"Oh. I don't think they even know about the shack yet, Gussie. Do you think I should tell them?" I looked up then and out to the road where I heard a truck. It was Martin. He pulled into the yard and drove to the barn.

"Uh, no. I'll check that shack out, Susan." Gussie dropped the wrench back on the ground and turned to me. He spoke quickly and more seriously than I'd ever heard him before. "I think you are getting to know so much that you might be dangerous to some people. So be careful. I'll check that shack out and let the police know what I find."

"Let me know too."

"Sure. For sure. But you stop taking any more risks. Andrew wouldn't like it." He picked up his wrench again and crawled back under the tractor.

Martin was out of the truck now so I didn't say anything more. But "Andrew wouldn't like it" didn't make much difference to me. Andrew didn't like a lot of things.

I smiled at Gussie's feet as I left to go to work. It was good to be able to talk to someone who listened and who was willing to help me. It was great to have someone think that I was all right, even smart.

CHAPTER ELEVEN

Martin spent most of the day fixing the pens in Andrew's barn. Gussie had the tractor running by noon and Fred drove it to the fields after lunch.

I worked through my chore list and had Andrew's supper simmering in the oven by quitting time. It had been a good afternoon. I'd listened to three new tapes on my Walkman without slowing down my work. I think I work better when I listen to music.

I fed Ruth a small bucket of hog-grower pellets. She looked lonely in the pigpen without the other pigs scrambling around her.

"She's unhappy," I'd told Andrew yesterday.

I'd been surprised when he agreed with me. "Oh aye, she's unhappy. She won't eat well when she's by herself. You'll have to talk to her, make her feel that she's not alone. But she still won't eat as well. Pigs thrive on competition for food. If she can have it all, she doesn't want it."

Today I paid more attention to her, giving her scraps and talking to her, but she didn't seem any better. I wasn't a pig so I wasn't good enough.

I tucked my Walkman in my jacket pocket, hung the earphones around my neck, turned the key on my bike and kicked the starter. First time. Lucky.

I was going to go home by the road, but it occurred to me that Gussie might not have looked over the shack, or he might not tell me about it in spite of his promise. I really should have a better look at it. There might be stolen goods there. There might be something interesting.

But this time I was going to be careful. I rode my bike halfway to the shack, then shut it off and pushed it the rest of the way. I stashed it in a clump of willows at the intersection of the main trail and the old logging road, then crept through the bushes the way I had this morning.

The woods looked different at this time in the afternoon. It was still daylight, but the shadows were longer and the light wasn't as bright. I don't know why, but it was at this point that I remembered how far away I was from any help. I wasn't planning on doing anything heroic; there shouldn't be any need to rescue me. The only real danger was bears.

I couldn't spend the rest of the summer worrying about bears. I'd be all right. There wasn't going to be anyone at the shack right now.

But there was. I saw the dark shape of the car as I crept through the trees at the last curve of the trail. A gray car. And a motorbike propped up against the shack near the door.

There were trees and the shadows cast by the trees close to the shack. I crawled through the bush until I could hear voices from the window.

Two people were arguing. I couldn't hear what they said, but I could hear the rise and fall of their voices in some kind of fight.

I squatted in the dark of the trees and thought hard.

I didn't want to get caught. That was the most important thing. The two in the shack were so busy with each other that they weren't watching for me. I was safe enough for the moment. I wasn't going to risk getting caught by poking my head in the door or even looking through the window. There were two of them and they were probably bigger, stronger and faster than I was.

My tape deck. It was a good one. Luke had given it to me for Christmas last year and it recorded as well as played. If I could get close to that window while the two inside were still arguing, I could put it on the windowsill and record what they were saying. I'd have to sacrifice the tape I'd made of my favorite record album, but it would be worth it.

I disconnected the earphones and left them hanging around my neck. I concentrated on the path to the window. There were a few dead branches to avoid, but as long as I kept low, I didn't think those two would either see me or hear me.

I took the tape deck from my jacket pocket and started crawling slowly toward the shack.

Now I could hear an occasional word. "I won't." That was Paul. The other person's voice was low, and I couldn't hear what he said. I worked my way closer, slowly and steadily. I was reaching up to put the recorder on the windowsill when I realized that I couldn't hear anything at all. I froze. Where were they?

"You'll have to lie low for at least two weeks." The voice was hard, commanding. And it was right above me. Whoever was there was looking out the window. I didn't move. I tried not to breathe. Had he seen me? My knees started to go weak, and I concentrated on staying just as I was, crouched against the wall of the cabin, one hand stretched up toward the windowsill.

"It's that girl. She knows too much."

Oh, great. Now they were after me. I wouldn't have a lot of chance to get away if they found me. What did I want to come here for? What a crazy thing to do! I wished I'd never thought of it.

"Oh yeah . . ." The voice faded as the man moved away from the window.

I had to get out of here. I set the "record" button, inched the small rectangular tape deck onto the windowsill and slid along the side of the cabin to the trees at the corner. I wasn't going to cross any open space that could be seen from that window. I crawled back into the trees like a snake to a hole, got to my feet as soon as I was out of sight of the shack and ran for my bike.

I was so afraid the two in the cabin would hear me that I pushed it almost to Evelyn's place. I was almost as afraid they'd decide to leave and catch me pushing the bike. Between worrying that they'd hear me and worrying that they'd catch me, I was shaking and sweating by the time I got to Evelyn's, and I had stomach cramps. I'm not built for this kind of danger. My body says, "Don't do it. I can't stand it." I went to bed.

But in the morning I had to go back for the tape deck. For one thing, Luke had given it to me and I didn't want to lose it. And for another, it might have recorded something valuable. If I could get proof that someone else was mixed up with Joe Stone, then both Martin and I might be cleared.

Someone else. I thought about the voice at the window. There was something familiar about it. Had I heard it before? Or did it just remind me of someone I knew—someone back home even? Why couldn't I place it? I gave up. Maybe when I heard the tape . . .

I spent the ride to the shack convincing myself that no one would be there. Even so, I shut the engine off early and pushed the bike most of the way. There was no car. Paul's motorbike was leaning against the shack. I wanted to run right then. But I wanted my tape deck even more. I ground my teeth and worried in the trees for ten minutes. In that time, I could have crawled up to the shack and grabbed the thing. What kind of a nut was I? Either I went for it or I didn't. I had to make some kind of decision. It was like standing on the end of a high diving board. You didn't know why you were stupid enough to be out there in the first place and you were afraid to jump, but you didn't want to waste all the courage it had taken to get there. Finally I crept through the trees, crawled up to the shack and snatched the tape deck off the windowsill. I shoved it into my jacket pocket and ran back to my bike.

It was easier to ride along the trail this morning. Everything felt more normal in the bright sunlight. Maybe Paul was still sleeping. Maybe he had left his bike there and gone off in the gray car last night. I hadn't seen anyone, but even so I didn't stop my bike until I was safely at Andrew's place. He was still in the yard working on something in the engine of his truck.

I parked my bike behind the barn and only then took the recorder out of my pocket and looked at it. I stared at it for two minutes before I realized what I'd done. When I set it on the windowsill, I'd pushed "record" but I'd also pushed the "pause" button. Instead of recording the conversation and shutting off when the tape was through, the tape deck had sat on the windowsill all night recording absolutely nothing and running its batteries right down. Not only did I have nothing on the tape, the batteries were dead.

How could I have been so stupid? How could I have been so incredibly stupid! I tried to remember how I'd set the tape deck. I'd done it quickly because I was so afraid I'd be caught. Great. Wonderful. All that risk for nothing. I might as well tell Andrew about the shack. He could tell the police. I couldn't protect Martin from his problems forever, and the police would learn about the shack from Evelyn or Gussie soon anyway. I wouldn't tell Andrew about the tape though. Too stupid.

CHAPTER TWELVE

I didn't expect a visit from the police after Andrew told them about the shack. I didn't want one either. I thought they would check the place out, and I'd never hear about it again. But the next evening Corporal Ferrier and a second officer came to Evelyn's place to talk to me.

"How did you know that there were two men in the shack?"

"Because I heard two different voices."

"What did they say?"

"I couldn't hear what they said. I could just hear them talking."

Corporal Ferrier stood, then walked in front of me. He was at least as tall as Allan. The other policeman stayed seated. He was shorter than the corporal, but broad like a football player.

Evelyn leaned back against the counter, her arms folded in front of her, listening, watching.

Ferrier looked down at me. I felt like a mouse cornered by owls.

"Your fingerprints were on the windowsill."

"I put my recorder there."

"Do you have a record of that conversation?"

Now I was going to look silly. I hesitated but finally told them the truth.

"No. I pushed the wrong button. I didn't have anything on the tape when I went back."

They looked at each other and then back at me.

It was then that I realized I had no proof of anything I'd done, that the police probably thought I was lying.

"Nothing on the tape?" Ferrier clicked the end of the ballpoint pen he was using. Click. Click. Click. I clenched my teeth. What would happen if I screamed at him to stop? I didn't scream.

"What does it matter anyway? I was there. I didn't stay."

"You reported the place to Andrew and so to us. What did you expect us to find there?"

"About what you found at Joe Stone's place. Stolen radios—that kind of thing."

"And we did. The same as Joe's place. Stolen radios and a body."

"A body!"

My hands were suddenly cold and the hair

rose on my arms. A body in the shack. Another murder? Who was doing this? Why couldn't the police find out who was doing it? There was a killer out there, and my fingerprints were on the windowsill.

"You recognize this man?" Corporal Ferrier pushed a black and white glossy photo towards me. It was the same jacket, the same T-shirt, the same long hair. I glanced at the face. He looked as though he was sleeping.

"Paul," I said.

"How well did you know him?"

I looked at Evelyn, then looked away and caught a movement at the dining room door. I could see Martin's reflection in the glass of the door.

"I saw him at the shack yesterday afternoon." My mind clicked along so fast I thought my head would shake. If I told them I met Paul at Andrew's place, they'd want to know what he was doing there. I'd have to tell them he'd come to see Martin, and that would get Martin into trouble.

"And I met him once near Andrew's."

"And?"

"And nothing. He stopped me and he was a jerk. He biked off."

"Nothing more?"

"I didn't even know his last name."

"Gibbons. Paul Gibbons."

Martin sidled in through the doorway and stood near his mother. Ferrier turned and studied him for a second. "Know this boy?"

He shoved the picture at Martin.

Evelyn grabbed the photo. "Of course he knows him. He went to grade school with him; you just told us it was Paul Gibbons. No secret about that. He was a pain, that boy. His mother tried when he was young—my, how she tried. Poor thing."

I wasn't sure if Paul or his mother was the "poor thing"—his mother, I think. Evelyn wouldn't waste much sympathy on Paul.

"Well?" Ferrier asked Martin.

"Yeah . . . like Mom says, I knew him."

"Seen him lately?"

"A couple of days ago. Don't hang around with him anymore. He was a loser."

"What kind of a loser?"

Martin shrugged. "Just a loser."

"When did you see him last and where?"

"He stopped at Andrew's. I told him I was working and I didn't have time to talk. So he left."

"Why did he stop to see you?"

Martin looked at the floor. "Didn't have nothing better to do, I guess. I don't know."

Ferrier took the photo back and put it on the table. He turned to me. "Tell me again why you were at the shack."

I'd already told him. This wasn't an information-gathering exercise here. The police suspected me of murder. I closed my eyes and took a deep breath. I felt a jolt and looked beside me. Evelyn had pulled up a chair and was sitting with me facing the police.

"You asked her that before. Do you think she killed Paul Gibbons?"

Ferrier stiffened. "We are only trying to get information."

"I couldn't have killed him. He was much bigger than me and a lot stronger. He'd have wasted me."

"He was poisoned."

"Oh." Great. He was poisoned. A weakling could have poisoned him.

"With what?" Evelyn asked.

"Alcohol and barbiturates. It doesn't take much of that to kill a man."

"So, are you accusing Susan of murder?"

"Look." Ferrier was tired. "I appreciate that you feel you have to help Miss George. But how about helping us?"

"If you have anything new you want to ask, go ahead. Otherwise, leave her alone."

"We'll ask her the questions we need to ask. Don't interfere."

"I'll interfere when I think I should. You don't badger a sixteen-year-old girl living here without her parents. Not in my kitchen you don't."

"Not in my kitchen!" Would it be okay with Evelyn if they badgered me outside in the yard? Anywhere else would be okay? I bit my lip to keep from giggling. It would be so dumb to giggle.

"Listen, Mrs. Lee. We won't harass her."

"No, you won't. In fact, you won't ask her

anything more unless Andrew is here too."

The other policeman got to his feet. Ferrier looked at him, then nodded. "Okay. We don't want anyone to accuse us of forcing information out of her. Okay. Okay." He faced me. "We'll talk to you with Andrew or with your lawyer. We'll call ahead when we want you."

I sat perfectly still. Why did I need a lawyer? I wished I'd never come to the Cariboo.

The door flew open with a thud and Fred stomped into the room. "What's with the police car? What's Martin done now?"

Evelyn flew to her feet like a boxer at the bell. "Nothing. Martin has done nothing. It's Susan the police want to talk to. And she hasn't done anything either. Honestly, Fred!"

"What is all this?" Fred turned to the two policemen who were trying to get out the door.

"We just wanted to ask Miss George some questions. We've discovered a cache of stolen property and the body of Paul Gibbons."

"Where?"

"In a shack on your property."

"Where on my property?"

"Near the south meadow, Fred," Evelyn said. "Remember I told you about finding that place?"

"Oh, yeah. That's right. Gibbons? Paul Gibbons? Isn't that one of your deadbeat friends, Martin?"

"Thanks, Dad."

"Fred." Evelyn's voice was sharp. "Paul hasn't been Martin's friend for years. Now mind your tongue."

"All right. All right. Can you guys get by my truck okay?"

"No problem," the broad-shouldered policeman called back. So he could talk. His silence worried me. I think he was the sergeant.

There was quiet in the room for ten seconds after the door closed on the police.

Then Fred exploded. "So! You've got yourself mixed up in a murder!" I looked up, almost terrified. How could I have prevented this? And why was Fred coming down on me? But he wasn't looking at me, he was looking at Martin.

"You think I don't know about your stealing, but I do all right. The probation officer told me about the charge. You shoplifted, but that wasn't good enough. Just peanuts that, eh? Now you're into the big time. Wholesale stealing. And what do you have to do with this murder?"

"Fred, how can you?" Evelyn grabbed Fred's arm although he hadn't tried to hit Martin. He didn't need to. Martin looked as though he'd been slugged with a bat. No one said anything for a second. Then Martin turned and walked through the dining room and out the front door.

Evelyn stood over the sink looking down at her hands. I just stared at Fred.

He finally looked at me. "What's the matter with you?"

I didn't answer. He turned to Evelyn. "What's the matter with *you*? Is everyone crazy around here? Martin's got to face himself. I'm only telling him what's good for him. And I've got a right to talk to him any way I like."

"You have no right to use your anger like a weapon against him or against me. I don't want a husband who is a lousy father."

"I don't want a wife who mollycoddles her son."

"Then you've got some decisions to make, haven't you, Fred? I come with a son. What are you going to do?"

"You'll do as I say!"

I got up and started for my room. Fred was something I couldn't handle. Then I remembered Evelyn pulling up a chair beside me and facing those cops. I turned back and walked over to the sink.

"You okay?"

She didn't look at me. But for the first time since I met her, I saw tears on her cheeks.

"You want me, Evelyn?"

She shook her head. "Thanks." She looked up, and her eyes were soft with tears. "I guess this problem isn't yours. You'd better call Andrew about your troubles." Fred was still standing in the middle of the room, bewildered, belligerent. "I'll be okay."

"I'll look for Martin," I said.

Evelyn brightened. "Thanks."

"Leave Martin alone. You let that weak-kneed excuse for a son face me by himself. He's always running away from responsibility."

No one answered him. I left by the front door. Evelyn was still standing at the sink with her back to Fred.

CHAPTER THIRTEEN

It was dark when I picked up my bike. I'd heard Martin leave when I was in the kitchen. I didn't know where he was going, but there weren't that many places to go around here. He'd either be at Andrew's place or in town. If he wasn't at Andrew's, I wasn't going all the way to town. I hesitated a few moments. There was a killer out there somewhere who had tried to run me off the road once. Would he be out tonight? I looked back at the Lees' house. I could stay there in safety. But Fred and Evelyn were sure to be fighting, and I'd promised Evelyn I would look for Martin. Besides, I'd rather be doing something than sitting in my room waiting.

I kicked the starter alive—first time—and wheeled out of the yard.

There was no one on the highway. No cars, no people, no bears. The porch light at

Andrew's house threw a pale light onto the gravel by the door. No lights showed inside the house. Andrew's truck was gone. He was probably over at Judith's. I circled the yard slowly and saw Martin's bike leaning against the side of the barn.

We hadn't left any sheep sick or ready to lamb. Why would he go to the barn now? I dismounted, shut off the motor and left my bike beside Martin's.

There wasn't any light in the barn. What was Martin doing in the dark? Maybe he was the killer? If he was, I was risking my life by going in there. No, he couldn't be. I knew that. At least, I thought I knew that. I wasn't sure of anything right now. I swallowed. This was ridiculous. I reached for the light switch and then stopped. If I switched on the overhead light, every sheep in the place would start to bleat. I stood at the doorway listening. I heard a sigh and then a thud. What was that? I couldn't help it; I had to see. If there was danger in this barn, I wanted to see it coming. I flicked the light switch and looked in the direction of the noise. A bench lay on its side, and beside the bench Martin was swinging and kicking and hanging by a rope from a beam.

The shock kept me immobile for a second. What an idiot! What a stupid idiot! Where was the knife? I'd cut open bales of hay for the sheep; where had I put the knife? On the windowsill. I moved. It was still there. I opened the jackknife, ran back to the center of the barn and righted the bench. Martin was still jerking, but I didn't dare look at his face. I'd read that people who hang themselves go a blue color, and their eyes and tongues stick out. I couldn't stand to look at that. So I wouldn't think of anything except what I was doing. The bench was a high one, so I could reach above Martin's head and saw at the rope. It took an eternity to cut. I kept my eyes on the rope and blocked my ears to the gurgling and gasping.

Sheep bleated and stamped and called for their lambs. I sawed at the rope.

At least he's still alive, I thought. Then he stopped making sounds and just jerked and kicked. "He's dead! He's dead!" The knife was dull, and I was afraid Martin would kick me and knock me down. I concentrated on sawing that blasted rope, and finally it gave. Martin slumped against me. I couldn't hold him and I couldn't keep my balance. He fell to the floor, and I fell on top of him. I was feeling for the rope around his neck as soon as we hit the floor, and I was mad.

"You idiot! You selfish brat!" I cursed at him as I struggled with the rope. I got it loose, but Martin didn't breathe. I pulled his head straight back, closed off his nose with my fingers and breathed into his mouth. I did that four times, and then his chest rose and fell and he took great gasps of air on his own.

I sat back on my heels and looked at him.

Tears ran down my face, and I just sat there and looked at him. He kept breathing. The sheep were crying for an extra feed.

After a few moments, Martin opened his eyes. His hand crept up to his throat. The rope was still there, but loose now.

"Susan?" he said. Then his face crumpled and he started to cry. "Why did you do that? Why aren't I dead?"

I was furious. I crawled around him and pressed his face between my hands. "You aren't dead because I cut you down!" I was hissing my anger at him. "And you aren't going to die because you'd hurt your mother so badly she'd never get over it. You got that straight, Martin? Whatever trouble you're in, you are not going to get out of it this way. You got that? You got that?" Now I was screaming at him. I shook his head and then let my hands drop. Martin hid his face in his hands.

I didn't feel sorry for him. "I'll feed the sheep. They'll quiet down."

I filled a bucket with whole barley and threw it into the troughs. Quiet settled over the barn. Except for the crunching as the sheep ate and the shifting for position at the trough, the barn was peaceful. I lifted the noose off Martin's neck and dropped it on the floor. Then I sat on a hay bale. "Okay, Martin, what's going on? Did you kill that Paul?"

He shook his head. "I didn't kill him. I

didn't kill Joe Stone either . . . but I was there when he died."

"You saw it? Who killed him?"

Again Martin shook his head. "You'd better not know. He'll kill you too."

"What happened at Joe's?"

Martin stayed where he was on the floor, half sitting, half lying. He spoke in a whisper, and I had to lean forward to hear him. "I was involved with that shoplifting gang, but I was trying to get out. I was, really. Only it was hard to leave. Joe told me he'd make sure I was planted with some stolen property if I tried to quit. And you know the next time I was caught, I'd get a jail sentence. My mom would hate that."

I nodded. "So he was blackmailing you?"

Martin looked up. "I guess so. Sort of. Anyway, I was there. And then the boss came."

"Who's the boss?"

Martin looked at me but didn't answer.

"What did the boss do?"

"He started to argue with Joe about the cut he was taking. See, the boss recruited the gang to do the lifting, and Joe took off the serial numbers and sorted the stuff. Then the boss hauled it away and fenced it in Kamloops. Joe got a cut, and he wanted a bigger one.

"I tried to leave a couple of times, but the boss was standing near the door, and I . . . I was afraid to go past him. So I stood back against the wall."

"So how did Joe get killed?"

"He started waving his arms and moving toward the boss. Joe always kept a loaded gun in the barn. He said he was afraid we'd come some night and steal from him, so he kept a small shotgun there. Everyone knew where it was. The boss just reached up and grabbed it and pointed it at Joe. Joe must have been crazy, he kept coming. The boss shot him. In the chest."

"Just like that?"

"Yeah. Joe didn't die right away. It was awful."

"And the boss?"

Martin stared at the barn wall, remembering. "He took the bottom of his shirt and wiped the fingerprints off the stock."

"What about you? Didn't he say anything to you?"

"Yeah."

"What?"

"He said if I ever told anyone, he'd kill my mother."

The sheep crunched on the grain. Whispers of hay slipped off the pile in the manger. It was peaceful here. I took a deep breath. "So you thought you'd kill yourself."

Martin nodded.

"That'd kill your mother for sure."

"He wasn't kidding, Susan."

We both heard the truck. Martin raised his eyes to the door and stared. If this was the killer, we were both dead.

It was Andrew.

"What are you two doing?" He looked at me sharply, at Martin, at the noose on the floor, then up at the beam.

He closed the door, walked across the barn to a hay bale and sat down. "Well, son," he said. "You need a hand?"

Martin looked at him and then away. "Thanks," he said.

I got to my feet and brushed the dirt off my jeans. "I'm going to phone Evelyn."

Andrew nodded. "Tell Judith I'll be in shortly."

"She's in the house?"

Andrew nodded.

"Okay. Evelyn will be over, I guess. Is there anyone else who could help?"

Andrew looked thoughtful.

"A friend? A girlfriend? Gussie?"

"No!" The word exploded from Martin. Andrew and I stared at each other. Gussie?

"Not Gussie." Martin was calmer. "Don't phone Gussie." His voice was only a whisper, but we could hear it plain enough. "I don't want everyone to know. Gussie would . . . Gussie would tell everyone."

"Okay," Andrew said. Martin looked back at the floor. I stood by the door staring at the bales of hay.

Gussie could have been at Joe's place the day he died. He had a car with the same letters on the license plate as the car that had tried to run me down. Gussie knew about the shack and didn't want me to tell anyone about it. Gussie was everywhere, knew everyone. And, most important, Gussie was the one Martin was afraid of.

Andrew stared at me over Martin's head. I nodded. It had to be Gussie. No wonder the voice at the shack had seemed familiar. And no wonder I couldn't place it: who'd ever connect Gussie with that cold, hard tone? Gussie, who always oozed kindliness and concern.

Judith was just starting out the door for the barn. Andrew had been gone long enough and she was worried. I told her what Martin had tried to do.

"Is he breathing regularly?"

I nodded. She was a nurse. She needed to know.

"No choking, no color change? I mean, his face and hands aren't blue?"

"He's all right. If we leave them alone, he might talk to Andrew."

Judith nodded. "Oh, yes. Andrew will listen."

It struck me then that Andrew *would* listen. He'd sit on that bale of hay and let Martin tell him anything at all. Would Allan listen that way? Maybe.

Martin was all right now. Andrew was in charge there. We had to do something. Ideas flitted around in my mind. I stared at Judith for a second.

"What I want you to do, Judith, is drive to Evelyn's place and tell her about it. She'll be less upset that way than if we tell her on the phone." I paused and thought over my plan. "Besides, I don't want anyone listening in on the party line."

"What do you have in mind?"

"I'll tell you when you get back. But listen, Judith." I grabbed her arm and made her face me. "Don't tell anyone but Fred and Evelyn what is going on here. In particular, don't tell Gussie. If he's at Evelyn's house, don't tell them about Martin."

"How can I not tell them?" She was exasperated.

"Just don't, Judith!" I shook her arm.

She nodded. "All right. I don't understand it, but all right."

"When you come back here, bring only one car and park it behind the tractor shed."

I wasn't sure yet how I was going to pull Gussie into a trap, but ideas were perking. I might be wrong too—maybe Gussie was innocent. But I could still see Martin's face when I suggested calling Gussie. He had been afraid. His eyes had been wide, and he had looked suddenly and completely terrified. Martin had reasons for those feelings.

I sat in Andrew's kitchen and waited for the Lees to arrive. Judith had left the light above the sink on, and it lit a small circle near the window. The dark closed in around the house. I checked out pictures in my mind:

Andrew sitting on a bale of hay listening to Martin, Judith calming Evelyn, Fred yelling. Gussie. Gussie sitting somewhere thinking. What did a person like that think about? I couldn't imagine what Gussie would be thinking.

CHAPTER FOURTEEN

I heard the car pull into the yard and saw Judith drive in behind the tractor shed. Good. Evelyn tumbled out, Fred got out more slowly. I met Evelyn outside the barn and hugged her.

"All right," she said, "I'm calm."

"He's all right." We went in together.

Evelyn took a deep breath. "How are you, Martin?"

He was sitting on the floor where he had been when I left. Andrew was still on the hay bale but stood when Evelyn arrived.

"Okay."

Fred was inside by now with Judith behind him. "Stupid thing to do." Fred searched through his pockets for the cigarettes he no longer carried. "Couldn't have been dumber."

Evelyn turned on Fred. "Shut up, Fred! You just shut up!" She broke off abruptly and turned away. I stared. Fred was crying. Tears ran down his cheeks.

Martin said nothing.

I walked into the circle of people and sat on the bale. "I have a plan that needs everyone's help."

Martin glanced at me, worried. Evelyn gave me a little attention, but she moved toward Martin.

"Listen, everyone." I didn't know if they would believe me, but I had to try. "Gussie is behind Martin's problems and he's behind the murders too. I'm sure of it."

Fred was irritated, Evelyn puzzled. At least I had their attention now.

"Don't be silly." That was Evelyn.

"We have a chance tonight to trap him before he does anything else."

Fred shook his head and Judith started to protest.

Martin looked up at me. "Don't, Susan. He'll kill you too."

Everyone was quiet.

I stared right at Martin. "But if we don't help you, he'll kill you, won't he?"

"Not me." Martin's eyes turned slowly to Evelyn.

"Your mother!" Fred exploded. "That snake. He was threatening you with . . ." He was purple with rage. Suddenly I understood how Fred survived life. If he was upset, hurt, sad, uncertain, fearful—he got angry. Everything translated into anger.

Evelyn reached over and wrapped her arms around Fred's waist. He looked down suddenly and hugged her. Evelyn's arms shook then she trembled all over. It was as though pain was expanding inside her, making her whole body shake. Fred stroked her hair. "It's all right. It's all right." Then his voice changed. Became firmer. "We'll get that . . . We'll get him. What do you have in mind, Susan?"

He turned to me, hands at his sides now. Evelyn bit her lip, took a couple of deep breaths and stood straight. "Yes, what can we do?" There was anger in the air, so much anger that I could almost hold it in my hands.

Judith moved forward. She looked at the noose on the floor. "Let me help too."

"How long will it take Gussie to get here after I phone him?" I was looking at Andrew, but Fred answered.

"About twenty minutes. He lives on the other side of the lake."

"How long will it take the police to get here?"

Martin started to speak, looked around at the group of determined people and changed his mind.

"About ten minutes," Evelyn offered.

"If we phone the police first, we can be sure they'll be here before Gussie. But if we do that, we run the risk of him overhearing our call on the party line.

"So we have to phone Gussie first. We give

him two minutes to leave his place, then phone the police and hope they get here in time."

There was silence when I finished outlining the plan. Fred looked at the ground, then slowly nodded.

"And if the police don't come?" Judith looked at Andrew.

"They'll come," Andrew said. "I'll call."

"Great." That would save me an extra five minutes convincing the police that we needed them. If Andrew insisted, they'd come.

Judith joined Andrew and me as we walked toward the house. "I'll leave those three alone for a few minutes."

"Do you think Fred will talk to Martin?" I didn't believe it.

"He'd better." Andrew was firm. "If he doesn't, I'll talk some sense into him."

I sat staring at the phone in Andrew's kitchen. I've never been an actress and I had to make this call convincing. I'd asked Andrew and Judith to sit in the living room because I didn't want them to hear me and I didn't want to be distracted when I was talking to Gussie.

I dialed his number. What if he wasn't home? Or had company? Or for some other reason couldn't come?

"Hello, Gussie? This is Susan . . . . Well, not so good. I'm at Andrew's. He's out, gone to Judith's, I think and . . . and . . . I found Martin Lee in Andrew's barn. What do I do?

I don't want to just leave and I don't want to be the one to tell Evelyn. I just couldn't tell Evelyn . . . . Yeah . . . . Yeah. He's dead all right. He hung himself. I . . . I . . . cut him down, but he's been dead quite a while."

I had to sound more upset. I tried a couple of fast breaths as if I was crying. "He . . . he . . . might have left a note for his mom, but I haven't looked. I don't know what to do. I guess you'd better call the police. There's my tape too . . . . The one I left at the shack last night. You know, I told you about the shack? Well, I rode past it last night, and there was a car parked beside it and a motorbike, so I left my recorder on the windowsill. I picked up the recorder tonight. I haven't listened to it yet, but it might tell us why Martin . . . why he did this . . . .

"Oh, great, would you? I'd be really grateful. I don't seem to be able to do anything but sit beside Martin. He was such a . . . nice . . . kid. I don't understand . . . . Thanks, Gussie. I'll wait in the barn."

Andrew and Judith were standing in the living room doorway. I clenched my teeth and nodded. "We got him!"

Andrew reached past me and dialed the police number. "Ferrier? Good. Andrew Ross here. I want three men out here in five minutes." Judith and I listened while he explained the situation to the police. I timed him. It took two minutes.

We ran back to the barn. The Lees were

sitting on the hay bale holding hands. Martin was in the center, and if I hadn't been so excited and so busy, I'd have told them how glad I was for them.

"Martin, you lie behind the bale. Judith, over there behind the feed sacks. Fred, you need to be where you can get out quickly. How about behind the equipment table? You'll have to crouch . . ."

"That's okay. I can see from there without being seen."

"Andrew, you have to be near the light switch."

At that point I heard a car in the driveway. Andrew shut off the light and peered into the night. "Police."

I checked my watch: seven minutes.

There were three of them, big men in uniform.

Andrew showed them where to park their cars and they were inside the barn in one minute. I told them briefly what we expected. "You three can hide in the sheep pens with the sheep. Gussie won't notice you there."

"And where are you going to be?"

"Right here where he expects me to be. Beside Martin."

Ferrier checked our positions. "Not so good. Fred, you go with my men. I'll take your place."

Fred, for once, did as he was told.

"No heroics," Ferrier said. "You don't have any guns here, do you?"

We shook our heads. "You do, I hope?"

"Yes, we do. But I don't want to be worrying about anyone else throwing ammunition around."

"No. No guns."

"Andrew? What lights will we leave on?"

"The one over the hay there. It will give him enough light to see you but not enough to show up the rest of us."

"Okay. Let's shut off the rest now." We took our positions. Martin lay on the floor behind the hay bale. I sat on it in front of him.

With the dark came silence. No one moved or spoke. I knew they were there, but I couldn't see them or hear them. I felt alone in the barn, waiting for the killer.

I imagined each of them in place. They were still there. No one had disappeared. Martin looked like a bundle of clothes on the floor.

We waited.

I checked my watch: seventeen minutes since I'd phoned Gussie.

"He's here." That was from Andrew. He was closest to the barn door.

I looked down at my hands and took a deep breath. Then I remembered the tape deck. It was in my jacket pocket. Where had I put my jacket? There it was on the floor. I dashed over, grabbed it and ran back to the bale. I could hear Gussie's car pulling up to the barn. Where was the tape deck? There. I fished it out and put it beside me on the bale. Martin was propped up on his elbow watching me.

"Down!" I whispered frantically. He dropped back to the floor.

Outside the barn, the engine stopped. I let out a long deep breath and waited.

CHAPTER FIFTEEN

A sheep bleated. Several stomped their feet and rustled against the boards of the pens. The rope Martin had used was lying on the floor beside me. Martin was stretched out immobile behind the bale. Everyone was in place. Gussie opened the door.

"Susan? Susan, how terrible!"

I looked at him as he leaned against the door. He seemed concerned, sympathetic, friendly. I'd always liked Gussie.

"Are you all right?" He started toward me. I didn't want him too close.

"I just listened to the tape, Gussie. You were at that shack last night."

He stopped. "What did you hear?"

"I heard your argument with Paul. I heard quite a lot." I flipped my hand toward the recorder on the bale. "It's all on tape."

"Is it now? That's too bad." He rocked back on his heels looking at me. He was just the same as he'd always been, friendly, half smiling. It was scary; he seemed so normal.

He reached into his jacket pocket and pulled out a gun—a small, black pistol.

"So you heard everything we said? And you haven't told anyone yet?"

I swallowed quickly. He was planning to kill me now. I didn't want him to try it too soon, before he'd talked quite a lot. I pretended not to understand his reasoning.

"You killed Paul and Joe and you . . . and you . . . drove Martin to this. How could you do so much harm?" I looked straight at him. If I pushed him, would he shoot me or would he talk more? "And you're not even very smart." I held my breath, but he laughed.

"Oh, I'm smart enough. Smart enough to keep a dozen teenagers shoplifting for me regularly. Smart enough to kill Joe Stone right in front of that useless kid there."

"Martin was there when you killed Joe Stone?"

"Right there. And the police think you did it. Now which one of us is smart?"

"And Paul? Why Paul?"

"You're surely not grieving for that waste of humanity, are you? He was a loser, was Paul. Greedy too. If you've got it all on tape, you know why I killed him. He wanted too much money from me. Didn't you hear that?" He was suspicious now, moving closer.

I nodded. "I heard it, but it seems an odd reason to kill someone."

Gussie stood straighter and frowned. "It's not odd. It's perfectly reasonable. And simple. He just wanted too much money."

"I didn't hear how you killed him. The tape ran out."

Gussie shrugged. "Oh, that was easy. I gave him a drink—good Scotch too—and laced it with barbiturates. He'd never had a good Scotch and he thought it was supposed to taste like that. Stupid kid. It would have been great to have you blamed for that one too, but I couldn't think of any way to do it."

"My fingerprints were on the windowsill."

Gussie roared with laughter. "Wonderful! Just wonderful. The local police won't look any further. They will be so glad to have a scapegoat handy, someone from outside the community, someone who doesn't belong, that they won't look one step further. They aren't very smart either."

I heard a movement from the sheep pens and waited for a second barely breathing, but Gussie seemed to accept the noise as normal.

"Well, now, you've really handed me a gift. Here you are in the barn with Martin's body. Perfect. All I have to do is shoot you and press Martin's fingers around the gun. The police will assume that he shot you and hung himself in remorse. Poor Martin. Such a loser."

This time the noise was unmistakable. Evelyn gasped. Gussie whirled toward the noise. Andrew flicked on the overhead light. I dove for the floor just as the noise of the exploding shell filled the barn. Martin was on his feet, a pitchfork in his hand. Gussie stared at him, his jaw slack, his hand limp, the gun pointing at the floor. Ferrier grabbed him from behind and jerked the gun from his hand. The other policemen surged over the pen divider and the three of them surrounded Gussie.

From the floor, everyone looked huge—Gussie a round blob like a potato puppet, the police in their uniforms like huge trees, Martin as thin and tall as bamboo, and Fred, Evelyn, Andrew, a wall around Gussie.

Ferrier snapped handcuffs onto Gussie's wrists. Gussie looked awkward with his short arms pinned behind him.

"I am arresting you for the murder of Joe Stone. It is my duty to inform you that you have the right to retain and instruct counsel without delay. Do you understand?"

We were silent, watching. Gussie said nothing. The flurry of action in the last minutes had left us all breathless, frozen. We didn't really know what to do next. Everything had stopped. We waited for Gussie to say something.

He paid no attention to Ferrier or the other policemen. He stared at Martin. "She said you were dead."

"She lied," Martin said.

Gussie looked down, then up again and slowly around at all the faces staring at him.

"You were all here." He looked at me. "It was a trap."

I stood by the rope and the hay bale. "It was a trap," I agreed. I faced him somehow but my knees were shaking.

"I should have killed you with the wrench the day you were alone here."

I remembered that day. I had felt no fear of Gussie. I'd thought he was kind then, and helpful.

"You are not obligated to say anything. But anything you do say may be given in evidence." The words sounded solemn, like some kind of vow or judgment.

I took a deep breath and sat down suddenly on the hay bale.

"Why did you want to kill me then?"

"You knew too much. You were putting too many things together."

"And that night on the road?"

"I wasn't after you then. I thought you were Martin on his bike. If I'd known it was you and the trouble you were going to be, I'd have made sure I got you then."

"So everything would be fine if you had only killed me? All you needed to do to make the whole world right was kill another person?"

"They would never have caught me without you."

"Martin knew."

"Oh, Martin." He shrugged as if Martin was a bug he'd stepped on days ago. "I had him too scared to talk. I could wait to take care of him."

I was on my feet but I didn't move closer to him. "Then I suppose if Evelyn had figured it out, you would have killed her too? You'd have killed everyone you knew, one by one."

"None of them were important. You know that."

What a twisted mind! "Face it, Gussie, you're crazy."

"That's enough of that!" Ferrier said, pushing Gussie toward the barn door. "He's not crazy at all. Just egotistical and stupid."

In spite of everything he'd done, Gussie reacted to Ferrier's criticism. "I don't have to take that kind of talk from you. I'm a respected man in this community."

"Not anymore, Gussie."

"You won't be able to prove anything!"

Ferrier looked around the group. "With this many witnesses? I think so. Once we have you safely in jail, we'll get a warrant and search your house. I bet you kept records of your shoplifting business."

Gussie stared at Ron Ferrier. "A search warrant?"

Ferrier nodded.

There must have been lots of evidence at Gussie's place because he stopped protesting right then. He looked at Martin once, then at me, then down at the barn floor. He said nothing more as they took him out.

We stayed in the barn waiting to hear the police car pull away. It stopped outside the barn and Ron Ferrier poked his head in the door. We were standing as he had left us. "Come down to the station tonight. I need affidavits from all of you."

"All right." Andrew moved toward the door.

"And Susan," Ferrier called over to me, "that was good. That was very good."

I nodded. It didn't feel good.

Ferrier left and I leaned against the wall. My knees were shaking again. I wasn't sure they were still controlled by my brain because I couldn't stop them shaking.

"Are you okay?" Martin was whispering. His throat must hurt. The skin was bright red with a blue welt where the rope had bruised it. At least I'd saved Martin. I started to feel better. And Gussie deserved everything he was going to get. And he would have killed me.

Evelyn stood beside me. "Thanks, Susan."

"No problem." I watched a ewe shake hay away from her face. Her jaws moved rhythmically as she chewed. "But it was ugly, wasn't it?"

Evelyn nodded, took my hand and led me over to the hay bale. We sat, holding hands.

Andrew had shut the barn door after

Ferrier and come back to the circle. Judith moved closer to him and they stood beside Fred, watching Martin, Evelyn and me.

"Martin has something to tell you, Fred." Andrew jerked his head in Martin's direction.

Fred looked wary but nodded. "All right."

Martin bit his lip but started to speak, croaking sometimes, but managing.

"I was mixed up with Gussie, I guess you know that now."

Evelyn nodded. Fred said nothing.

"Well, I did some shoplifting for Gussie. Just a couple of times, and I got caught and got community service and I told Gussie I wouldn't do it anymore. But . . . but he told me that I had to, that once I was in his gang, I couldn't stop. He told me that I was smart enough to do it and not get caught. But I didn't want to. Mom thought I'd never do it again and I just *couldn't*." No one said anything. Some hay rustled in the manger as a sheep looked for more food. Andrew held Judith's hand but neither said a word.

Martin continued. "But I did. I stole twice more and then I couldn't handle it. I called Gussie and he told me to meet him at Joe's. I thought maybe he was going to let me off. Joe didn't think I was any good, and I thought maybe he'd told Gussie that. But they were arguing when I got there. Joe was the one who filed off all the serial numbers and altered all the hot stuff so the police couldn't trace it. He was working on some stereo equipment and said he thought he should get paid more. They were always arguing about money."

Martin cleared his throat and went on. "Anyway, Gussie got sarcastic and that made Joe mad. He started waving his arms and screaming at Gussie. I backed into a corner. Joe started quoting the Bible, stuff about 'the wages of sin' and 'olive trees' and 'vipers.' And he kept coming closer. Gussie picked up the .410 that Joe kept by the door and just shot him. Just like that. One minute Joe was yelling and jumping around, the next minute he was dying. I don't think Joe would've hurt Gussie. I think he just liked to yell and scream a lot, but Gussie shot him."

Martin's voice was a soft whisper, but I heard every word.

CHAPTER SIXTEEN

"What did you do then?" Andrew's voice was gentle. I'd never heard him speak so softly.

"I stared at Gussie and watched him clean the stock with his shirt. Then I think he remembered I was there. He said, 'Here, catch,' and threw the .410 to me. I caught it. I didn't think about it. I just caught it like you do when someone throws you a ball or something."

Andrew nodded.

"Then Gussie said, 'Too bad you had to kill him.' "

" 'Me?' I stared at him. 'I didn't kill him.' "

" 'You're holding the gun,' Gussie said and then he left."

"I dropped the gun and went over to Joe. He'd been hit in the chest and he wasn't dead yet. He looked at me, then his eyes went blank and he died."

"Oh, Martin," Evelyn was holding back her tears but she was almost choking on the effort.

"My fingerprints were on that gun. My fingerprints were in the RCMP files from that shoplifting charge. I was going to get nailed for murder." He was quiet for a moment, looking down at his feet. I knew how I'd felt when I thought the police suspected me of murder. Martin would have been sure they'd charge him. "I felt Joe's neck for a pulse the way they do on TV, but he was dead all right. So I wiped the gun clean and left it beside Joe. Maybe people would think it was suicide."

"So you went home," Andrew said, "and you told not a soul." He'd heard this before, I knew that; he was just trying to get Martin to tell us.

"I went straight home but I thought the cops would be after me."

"Why?"

"Because I met Judith on the road and she recognized me. She waved."

"But I didn't realize Joe died on that day. I didn't realize it until I came back from the south. Susan told me."

Martin shrugged. "I didn't know that."

"And when no police came for you?" Andrew was helping Martin keep his story organized.

"When no one came for me, well, then I

thought maybe I was going to be safe again."

Evelyn was swallowing hard and trying not to cry, and Fred stood as stiff as a mannequin.

"Then Mom found the shack and I knew that the radios were still there. I don't know, I guess I thought maybe that shack would disappear. Or no one would find it. I don't know what I thought. But once Mom found it, well, my fingerprints were on the radios. I don't know how long fingerprints last. I've heard that sometimes they can last a long time if the weather is dry and the prints are good. I stacked the radios in there. I didn't steal all of them, some Paul brought and some the other kids stole, but I knew my fingerprints would be on a lot of them.

"Everything was closing in on me again. Then the cops came and it seemed like they were going to pin Paul's murder on Susan. I knew who must've killed him. Gussie didn't care about people. And now if Susan was getting charged with murder I should do something about it. But I couldn't—couldn't do a thing about it. I couldn't see how I'd ever be free of it. Always there'd be something pushing me. So I figured I was better off out of the whole mess and everyone else would be better off too. So that's why . . ." He nudged the rope with his foot.

Fred stood in the same position, ramrod straight, tears on his cheeks. "I . . ." He hesitated, cleared his throat and tried again.

"I'm not very good at talking," he said. There was silence. No one moved. "I'm . . . I'm sorry, Martin."

I was afraid to move. The words seemed like some kind of magical incantation hanging in the air. I don't suppose Fred had ever said that before in his life.

Martin raised his head and looked at his dad.

Fred pulled out his handkerchief and blew his nose. His voice was gruff. "Nice kettle of fish your mother and I would be left with. How did you expect us to live with the fact that you'd killed yourself?"

"Yeah, Andrew told me. I'd be out of the mess but you'd be in it for the rest of your lives."

Fred snorted. "Besides," he said, sounding like the old Fred, "it'd be damned dull around the place with you gone. No one to yell at."

Martin's face softened a little. "Yeah," he said, "I can see you'd have a problem." And he smiled.

"Now." Andrew had had enough sentiment and wanted to get things on a firm footing. "Where do we go from here?"

"It's easy to see where we go from here." Fred was emphatic. "Martin says he can't live with all this. Well, he's right. He shouldn't live with it." Fred absentmindedly hunted through his shirt pockets for cigarettes again. "Martin has to go to Ferrier and tell him the whole thing."

"But the radios?" Martin was worried.

"You stole some of them, didn't you?"

Martin sat up slowly. "Yes, sir."

"You'll have to take whatever punishment the courts dish out. Got that straight?"

"Yes, sir."

Evelyn protested. "Fred, everything isn't black and white. You aren't always right."

Martin quieted her. "He's right this time though, Mom." His voice was low and he looked lost. If I could have gone in his place right then, I'd have done it.

"And I'll go with you," Fred said.

Stiff-necked, proud and nasty-tempered as Fred was, he was going to stick by Martin. I should have known that the grouch would be reliable. He was like a cactus in the desert— prickly and ugly but he stood the weather well.

Andrew leaned forward. "Martin, is that what you want to do?"

"I guess it's the only way."

"We'll go home now, son."

"What about the police station?" Judith interjected as Fred turned toward the door.

"Yeah." I remembered Ferrier's directions to us. "We're supposed to show up there to give our information."

"We'll show up there at seven in the morning. You three will keep the police busy enough for tonight. In any case, I'm not going down there any earlier. Ferrier can wait."

"Make it eight, Dad. I have to do chores here in the morning."

Fred blinked, looked at Martin and nodded. "Sure, okay. Eight. Tell him eight."

Evelyn squeezed my hand and then the three of them left together.

"Well." Andrew looked around the barn and then back at Judith and me. "What are you waiting for, women? If we have to go to the police station, we'd better get going unless you two want to be up all night."

"Are we holding you up, Andrew?" I grinned at him as I passed.

"Don't be brash," he said and switched off the barn light behind us.

CHAPTER SEVENTEEN

We drove to the station in Andrew's truck, the three of us in the cab high above the road. The ride was smoother above the truck springs than it was on my Honda.

Ferrier was waiting for us. We gave him Fred's message. He grunted but didn't object more than that.

"Please sit down." He pointed to some chairs, the old wooden kind with polished, curved arms that I used to see in odd corners at my high school. A constable sat at a desk in the corner, but Ferrier didn't introduce him, and while he nodded at us, he didn't speak. Corporal Ferrier had taken off his brown jacket and his tie. He looked harassed and bone tired.

"Try to tell me everything as you remember it, starting when you first found Martin tonight."

I wasn't going to tell him everything.

Martin should be the one to tell him about the stealing. How did I get into these situations where I wanted to do the easy thing, the straightforward thing that wouldn't be quite the right thing? I had to tell Ron Ferrier everything he needed to know about Gussie, but nothing that Martin was going to tell him the next morning.

It took a lot of thinking. I had to be alert so that it wouldn't be obvious I was leaving some things out. I didn't want to tell any lies either. I felt as though I was dancing on ice, and I was really tired when I finally finished the story.

"So you really weren't sure that Gussie was the man you wanted?"

I squirmed in my seat. This was the hardest wooden chair I'd ever sat on. "I wasn't sure with my head. I mean, I didn't have all the reasons I needed. But I was sure with my feelings."

"Oh." Ferrier looked at me as if I had lost half my brains. That annoyed me.

"Look, if a little kid comes up to you and stares at you, sometimes you know that he wants you to comfort him. Right?"

Ferrier shrugged. "I guess."

"My mother says that sometimes you know for sure something is so without even knowing why you know."

"I'd hate to make an arrest on that."

"No, you couldn't. But I bet you act on that all the time. Aren't you suspicious of some people and watch them just because you know they're going to cause trouble?"

"I suppose so."

"Okay. When I mentioned Gussie's name, I saw the look on Martin's face and I *knew* then that Gussie was the one."

"Just like that."

"Just like that," I said flatly. "Andrew saw it too."

Ferrier glanced at him. Andrew nodded.

After I'd finished, Andrew and Judith gave their statements. We had cups of tea while we talked, and the silent constable at the other desk wrote down everything we said.

"Come back tomorrow and sign your statements, all right?" Ferrier walked to the door with us.

We nodded. My teeth hurt. I slowly tried to relax my jaw muscles.

"And thanks again, Susan. You were a great help." We shook hands.

"And thank you for coming when you did," I said politely. Then I glanced at him quickly. This was a silly conversation. You'd have thought we'd come for a tour of the police station. "It was a pretty scary situation."

"Of course it was a scary situation. You can't set a trap for a murderer—as if you had four years of police college and an army behind you—and not have 'a scary situation'."

I stepped back. He wasn't friendly anymore.

"Sorry."

"You ought to be. How *could* you think we'd try to pin a murder on any innocent person, outsider or no outsider?"

He was really offended. Even hurt. "Sorry," I said again. This time I meant it.

"When are you heading back south?"

"At the end of the summer."

"Will we see you here next year?"

I glanced at Judith and Andrew. Would I come back? That depended on a lot of things. I hadn't thought much about Allan all the time I'd been in the Cariboo, but he was back in Chilliwack waiting for me. We had decisions to make.

"I guess I'll have to wait and see."

We were driving down the dark road back to the ranch when Andrew suddenly cleared his throat. It was so loud that both Judith and I jumped.

"Hey!" Judith protested. "You woke us up."

"Ah . . ." Andrew said. "Ah, if you are looking for work next summer, Susan, you haven't been doing such a bad job I wouldn't have you back."

I translated that in my mind to mean that he would be glad to have me working for him again.

"Thanks, Andrew. I'll keep it in mind. The trouble is . . ."

"The trouble is," Judith picked up my thoughts, "you don't know what you're going to be doing next year. Maybe you'll be back here in McLeese Lake, married and fighting roosters. And maybe you'll be flying a weekly commercial run to Singapore."

She had the right idea. "Neither of those things is going to happen in a year, Judith."

"No, but maybe in three years."

"I don't know."

It was amazing how they wanted me to belong. And amazing how I wanted to belong. I'd come here to be free of my family, free to make my own decisions. I wanted to be independent. I *am* independent, but I want to belong too. I guess I need to care about people. I'd only come for the summer and now I felt part of the community. And I'd started off such an outsider.

"The outsider," I said aloud.

"What's that?" Andrew's voice was sharp.

"I was just thinking that I am the outsider."

"Don't listen to that Gussie. You know he's crazy."

Dear Andrew, such a fraud. I snuggled my face into Judith's shoulder and drifted into a doze. Andrew was like an egg, hard on the outside, soft in the middle. And my friend.

I'd never judge a person by a gruff manner again. Even Fred had his good points.

"You be sure to come back now, eh?" Andrew shifted gears before a long hill.

"Whatever you're doing, we'll always want you back." Judith hugged me.

I smiled but I didn't answer. It felt good to be wanted but I couldn't promise anything. I'm not psychic. I can't read my future or anyone else's. Tomorrow's like the night out there: mysterious, secret, full of surprises. I might be anywhere, doing anything. Look at this summer. I couldn't have planned it. Anything might happen tomorrow. Just anything.

Printed in Canada